THE HENCHMAN

Kjell-Olof Bornemark

DEMBNER BOOKS • New York

DEMBNER BOOKS
Published by Red Dembner Enterprises Corp.,
80 Eighth Avenue, New York, N.Y. 10011
Distributed by W. W. Norton & Company, Inc.,
500 Fifth Avenue, New York, N.Y. 10110

Library of Congress Cataloging-in-Publication Data

Bornemark, Kjell-Olof, 1924–
    [Handgängen man. English]
    The henchman / Kjell-Olof Bornemark ; translated by
Laurie Thompson.
    p. cm.
    Translation of: Handgängen man.
    ISBN 0-942637-19-4 : $17.95
    I. Title
PT9876.12.O76H413   1990   89-27701
839.7'374—dc20   CIP

Handgängen Man, the original edition of this novel, was published by
Askelin & Hagglund, Stockholm.

The Henchman was translated from the original Swedish edition by
Laurie Thompson.

Design by Antler & Baldwin, Inc.

THE HENCHMAN

1 Every sound was exaggerated by the cold, which settled over the dozing city like an invisible but impervious dome. Bringing its full weight to bear on the evening, it threatened to smother and crush everything foolish enough not to seek shelter indoors. Smoke rising from the chimneys was forced back earthward to form dense, milky-white veils seemingly anchored firmly to the rooftops; the distance to the stars had been reduced by several light-years. The moon grew even bigger and brighter, glaring down with icy disdain at the snow-filled, almost deserted streets and squares. The planet Venus hovered ominously over the shivering citizens, many of whom feared it was on course to collide with the earth.

The ceiling and walls creaked, and the last few nights he had been woken up by noises that had driven him out of bed—he still could not find where they were coming from. He had started hearing sounds from the apartment next door, and realized his place was not as well insulated as he had imagined. While this gave him food for thought, it did not worry him. He knew full well it was not the cold making him

1

more conscious of his surroundings over the last week or so, but an increased awareness.

His apartment was on the very top floor of the block, and from the window Jonas Mikael Frey could see the blinking red and white lights of a private airplane coming in to land at Bromma Airport. Beyond there, on the other side of Jungfrudansen, he could make out the newly built, sterile, rectangular skyscrapers of Huvudsta, devoid of any trace of beauty but not without a certain cocksure dignity. In the far distance to the left, the pitch-black sky faded into a bluish haze, marking the limits of the glow and smoke generated by central Stockholm.

From no fault of his own, Frey had been condemned to ten days of partial house arrest. That was why he had been standing in the semidarkness by the window for over half an hour, waiting and listening. The television was switched off, and the only light came from a standard lamp in one corner of the room.

He was in a strange, almost undignified state. All week he had been struggling with suppressed anger that gradually and in spite of everything had given way to a resigned if surly state of waiting. By this evening, all that was left was vague and very insecurely based hopes.

In fact, he was not hoping for anything any more. Or rather, he was hoping that nothing would disturb his waiting, which is not the same thing, of course. That is why he was listening attentively to every noise coming from the staircase. He did not want to admit, not even to himself, that what he dreaded most was the asthmatic hissing noise from the elevator. That meant someone was on the way up. The elevator only went as far as the floor below his own, and it took fifteen seconds to reach it from the ground floor. If the final, despairing sigh came earlier than that, he could breathe again and wait for the next visitor to arrive. If not, there was nothing he could do but listen for footsteps climbing the stairs up to his floor, and hope that they were heading for his neighbor on the other side of the landing.

It was approaching eight P.M., the time when his watch came to an end for the simple reason that the entrance door was locked then. After that time, visitors without a front-door key were unable to get in. He was free to go down to the bar for a beer and a whiskey, and maybe also a little inane conversation to break the monotony.

For the first week of his enforced confinement, he had tried to prepare himself for what lay ahead. That would have been the rational thing to do if there had been something definite to latch on to. As it was, he had no idea of what was going on, and he had grown tired of guessing since all guesses would eventually prove to be unfounded or irrelevant.

Frey had been asked—or, rather, ordered in a fairly polite matter—to look after an unnamed guest and to provide him with bed and board. In addition, he was expected to cooperate with this unknown person and use all means at his disposal to assist him in his work and secure his safety.

Such a request might make anyone feel annoyed. As time goes by and nothing happens, the idea of what lies in store becomes increasingly uncertain and irritating. The very state of waiting becomes a vague threat. Only people lacking in imagination have no difficulty in banishing suspicions, and they are usually made to pay dearly for their lack of foresight.

The time Frey had been given was ten days. If no one appeared to take advantage of his assistance and hospitality in that time, he would consider himself relieved of all obligations and go back to his routine tasks. This was the slender lifeline to which Jonas Mikael Frey pinned his suppressed but daily more substantial hopes.

With just over twenty-four hours to go before that time was up, there was a microscopic chance that the people making the decisions in Berlin might have changed their plans at the last minute and resolved to exclude his parti-

3

cipation—they had indicated themselves that such a move was not impossible. If that really were the case, he would be able to breathe a sigh of relief and, paradoxically enough, feel safe and secure once more.

The paradox lay in the fact that Jonas Mikael Frey was the agent of a foreign power, and it was always assumed that people who did jobs of that kind would never be able to feel secure. Like many another statement that had not been properly thought through, it was both true and untrue. Even if security is only an illusion, there is no reason to exclude a single living soul from its deceptive allure. Even agents have their weaknesses and need to dream themselves out of the cold, unscrupulous reality that is not their realm alone, but one they share with all other living beings.

They had chosen a very complicated way of making contact with him. Indeed, the very means were sufficient to set the alarm bells ringing.

It had all started at The Redcoat, a bar in the center of Stockholm. It was hidden away in a back street on Kungsholmen, and there was little risk of him being seen there by anyone he wished to avoid. The waitresses and regulars had got used to him, and now treated him politely but without any great personal curiosity. Everyone took it for granted he was not looking for company, that he preferred to be left alone. He generally sat in a little alcove and retreated behind an evening paper while drinking his beer or nibbling at one of the German snacks the landlord was famous for.

It was unusually noisy in the bar that evening, and the sound level continued to rise steadily. Most of the noise came from an oval table that filled most of the middle of the room, where supporters of an ice-hockey team were intent on drowning their sorrows and washing away the shame of yet another ignominious defeat. The green club pennant drooped limply on its pole in the middle of the table, and it was advisable not to utter a word about ice hockey if one wished to avoid sparking off a row.

4

Farther away, in an area of the room partially hidden behind a partition, a dozen men sat huddled together, their voices by no means as loud but much more hoarse. Their conversation was not especially articulate and consisted mainly of grunted questions or statements that were always responded to in the same way. Their less-than-elegant winter garb indicated that most of them had taken early retirement, an impression reinforced by their faces, all of which displayed signs of constant defeat in the battle with alcohol.

Several of them had tried to make contact with Frey when he first started going to The Redcoat. They came one at a time, and it was obvious they were all looking for somebody new to talk to. They were hoping to find someone who was too polite simply to tell them to go away. Someone who, like themselves, was grateful for any break in the monotony and hence willing to listen to their dreary and relentlessly revealing stories. Such a conversation could give them a grain of self-respect, or at least give them cause to believe their self-pity was justified. Beer and spirits were no longer able to help them flee from a reality that held them in check like a scratch on a gramophone record, killing off the music by repeating the same bar over and over again until someone takes pity, lifts the needle, and puts an end to it all. Only their dreaming of the past—a fictitious and confused past—when they still believed they had a future, could console their despair.

They never entered into conversations like that without conditions: They—and only they—must be allowed to touch up the past in garish colors of their own choice. Their audience was required to remain silent above all, but also needed to display understanding and respectful interest bordering on the elimination of self. Hence, they would greet every interruption with a brusque: "Listen now! Let me finish!" The fragile framework of their castles in the air must not be torn apart. If they allowed chilly reality to intrude, the

5

illusion would dissolve in a puff of smoke and be replaced by an awkward and powerful smack in the face.

Jonas Frey had sent them all packing, politely but firmly. Ever since, he had been regarded without warmth by the regulars, but he was tolerated, and Frey had thus succeeded in his intention of merging into his environment without needing to play an active role in it. He no longer aroused any attention or curiosity at all when he went to the bar.

What the owner, customers, and staff did not know, however, was that The Redcoat had been chosen by Frey and his masters as one of a number of emergency contact locations. In a way, the bar was one end of a lifeline that would save Frey from shame and ignominy if ever lightning suddenly threatened to strike. A bolt from the blue is a rarity, not least in the world of espionage. Clouds tend to build up on the horizon, and you can hear ominous rumbles and see dazzling flashes, provided you are sufficiently wide awake and know how to interpret the signs.

During the three years Frey had been a regular customer at The Redcoat, no representative of the Insurance Company or its local branch had tried to warn him. Every time he left the bar after a few quiet hours, he had good reason to believe he was not on the point of being exposed. Things would probably be different if someone had tried to contact him there, of all places. Probably, but not necessarily.

Frey had always taken it for granted that he was being watched—not by his opponents but by his own side. The role he played was a significant one, and he and his organization were comparatively expensive; it would thus have been careless, or even indefensible, not to try and protect him. Even so, he had never noticed anything that might suggest his suspicions were justified. If he were being tailed, those persons knew how to make themselves invisible and had acted in a thoroughly professional manner. He also assumed these discreet guards had the subsidiary task of keeping an eye on him and, in so far as it was possible and advisable, not only to check the reports he was sending regularly to Berlin but also to report on his physical and mental state.

The funeral feast at the ice-hockey table, as was inevitable, had developed into a name-calling match that threatened to deteriorate any moment into a fistfight. It was time for Frey to leave The Redcoat. First, however, the two pints of beer he had drunk indicated a visit to the toilets.

When he came back, he noticed the signal when he was still five yards short of his seat. He started, and stood stock-still in the middle of the floor for a couple of seconds. Then he shook off the first, paralyzing feeling of terror. All was not necessarily lost. It was just that the threat had edged a little closer and was pointing a warning. Teeth clenched, he continued the few paces left to his seat. He looked a little more ponderous, more weary than before. Even before he got there, he had started talking to himself inwardly, without moving his lips, in order to cool down. Don't let yourself be tricked into panicking, don't be over hasty, don't do anything rash. Even so, he could not stop his face from flushing, and he started to sweat copiously.

The matchbox was lying on top of the packet of cigarettes he had left beside his lighter to indicate that the table was taken. It was a box advertising a Chinese restaurant not far from where he lived in Sundbyberg. Someone had placed it there during the short time he had been away. It was not just a coincidence. The label with the defiant two-tongued dragon, its two greedy tongues pointing at whoever looked at it, was all too familiar as far as Frey was concerned. He could still remember the desk to which he had been summoned in order to choose from among the various proposed signals. Both he and the Colonel were in good spirits after a few glasses of vodka. He had plumped for the dragon immediately, and the Colonel had laughingly urged him to watch out for the monster's two tongues.

"Both are deadly poisonous," the Colonel had said. "But there is an antidote for one of them."

7

Since that day, Frey had lived in the hope of never having to see again that ominous creature, seemingly capable of coldly and ruthlessly negating and eliminating everything in range.

Frey looked around him. Everyone seemed intent of following the increasingly rowdy behavior of the ice-hockey fans. When he had arrived at the pub an hour or so earlier, he had automatically scrutinized every face in the room. Most of them were familiar, and none of the few casual customers who were already installed or turned up later had aroused his suspicions.

Frey had left his parka hanging on the clothes rack located on one of the short walls, and when he went to retrieve some cigarettes from one of the pockets, he was confronted by two middle-aged men he could not place straightaway. Somehow or other, he was convinced he had seen them before. He dredged through his memory in vain, and soon gave up and returned to reading the paper. It was mainly their appearance that had struck him. The elder one was short and very slim, and wore trousers the likes of which Frey had not seen for years. Although they were made from the best-quality English wool, they looked for all the world like the trousers Russian men were forced to wear long into the sixties. The younger one had a chubby face and wore circular glasses that served to emphasize his chubbiness still more. The sleek, black hair and the slightly protruding cheekbones made him look almost Asian, an impression reinforced by his unusually warm smile, which was enough to put any observer off his stride. Either this man was retarded, or he was boundessly amused by the reality he had long since learned to control.

They made an odd pair, and Frey had difficulty in understanding why they continued to hold his attention. Their peculiar appearance ought to ensure that they would remain in the memory and be easily recognizable even months later. At the same time, they seemed strangely featureless, as if they might easily fade away into oblivion at any moment.

Brutal violence, like erotic games, has always been irresistible to human beings, especially if they do not need to take an active part in the goings-on and merely play the role of observer. When the first punch was thrown at the ice-hockey table, every customer in the bar froze and stared glassy-eyed at the same point. It was like looking at a Brueghel painting of Hell. It is only in art that time stands still, however, and the tableau soon fell apart. Several more pacifistically disposed friends managed to break the spell and separate the two combatants before any more damage was done.

The owner had been called and was on his way to the battlefield in the company of a hefty waiter. There was no chance of anyone not involved or merely curious paying any attention to what Frey was doing, and indeed, this was a necessary condition if his actions in the next few seconds were to have any point.

Frey was ready to receive the message. He would also acknowledge it, without being sure of who would pick up the receipt.

There were only a few matches in the box, and he pushed them aside with his finger so that he could read the message. It was brief, consisting of just a single series of figures:

16—16—66.

The code was easy for the initiated to understand. On the sixteenth of this month, at sixteen hundred hours, he was expected to take a meal at the Chinese restaurant named on the back of the matchbox. Of the numbered meals on the menu, he was required to order number sixty-six.

This meant he had almost twenty-four hours in which to prepare himself. At the same time, the message implied that he was in no immediate danger. It was not the police, nor the secret police—SÄPO—that were on his trail.

Whoever sent the message had brutally ripped open the veil of security and safety behind which Frey had been living these past six months. If the intention was to arouse the suppressed talents Frey was known to possess, it had been entirely successful. In the space of a few minutes, he was transformed into a cold-blooded, coolly calculating, efficient, and in every respect suspicious man. The Colonel had chosen the right way of priming the Swede for action.

The rush of adrenaline had begun to subside, and Frey started to feel thoroughly bad-tempered instead. A very long time ago, when he was still very young, a message of this kind would have made him aggressive, and his mounting excitement would have put him in a state verging on elation. He would have wandered around in a dream, impatient for his expectations to be fulfilled. Now, he did not even try to protect himself from his ill-humor. This did not mean he had become less competent or useful, however. On the contrary!

Without looking around, Frey took a cigarette from the packet and tried to light it with a match from the box in front of him. He failed, as he meant to do. He had better luck the second time, and he puffed a thick cloud of smoke through one side of his mouth. Then, he just sat there with the matchstick at eye level, allowing it to burn down to his fingertips before blowing it out with a powerful blast of air that left his face set in a grimace.

In doing so, he had signed the receipt and the messenger was duly informed. All that remained was for him to leave the bar. The row had subsided as suddenly as it had begun, the customers had come back down to earth, and muttered conversations were resumed.

Jonas Mikael Frey put on his parka and pulled his fur cap down over his ears. As he maneuvered his way through the tables, he looked querulous, as if he had a stomachache, and everyone could see he was far from happy.

When he emerged into the cold night, Frey walked briskly toward the underground station. He did not turn around at all, knowing to do so was pointless. They were presumably still watching him, but there was no reason to suppose they must be behind him. Shadows can be cast in all directions, and it is sometimes hard to catch up with them.

The young Chinese waiter looked quite uncomprehending when, after studying the menu carefully, Frey ordered number sixty-six.

"It's off," said the waiter. "We haven't got it. Never have had."

"But I've had number sixty-six specially recommended," repeated Frey emphatically but without raising his voice.

"I'm sorry. It's not possible. We don't have any dishes on the menu with that number. Try sixty-five instead. The duck. It's excellent."

There could be no question of linguistic misunderstanding. His vowels had the ring of a Stockholm dialect, and it was clear the young man had been born in Sweden.

"That's odd," muttered Frey, fully audibly. "I usually have a good memory for figures. But I'll settle for the duck."

For the next hour Frey sat there eating and drinking without anyone trying to engage him in conversation. By about five o'clock the restaurant was starting to fill up with customers from the nearby offices. A couple of police patrolmen called in to pick up take-out meals in foil-covered boxes. They were treated with meticulous politeness, and Frey did not see them pay at all.

After a few more minutes Frey decided he had had enough, called the waiter, and asked for the bill.

It was handwritten.

1/66	66:-
Wine	54:-
Coffee	8:-
Cognac	38:-
	166:-

The bill was on a little silvery tray, and carefully folded. To make sure it was not blown away, the waiter had thoughtfully placed a matchbox on top of the bill: Its label was identical with the one that had summoned Frey to the restaurant in the first place. He would have been surprised and somewhat put out if this friendly gesture had been overlooked. There was no need to open the box just yet—Frey knew what was in it. In among the matches would be a sealed matchsticklike capsule containing instructions.

He looked up at the Chinese, who was still standing at the table. This time, he was able to look the messenger in the eye, but there was nothing to be gained by doing so. The lad was nothing more than a hired telegram boy, and he would be totally nonplussed if Frey tried to start a conversation with him.

Without changing his expression Frey paid the bill and told the attentive waiter to keep the change. Only when Frey nonchalantly slipped the matchbox into his jacket pocket did the Chinese bow respectfully and leave the table with a satisfied smile.

Discomfort can be caused by all kinds of things. Sometimes it is a question of interaction between the stomach and the brain, or what for want of anything better we call emotions. Frey was in relatively good shape physically, but for a week or more his emotional state had been close to the freezing point. The reason for his discomfort was easy to explain. The method his masters had chosen to contact him emphasized the importance they attached to the business at hand. It was obvious they wanted to guard against any possibility of outsiders catching onto what was afoot. As far as possible, they wished to conceal their intentions. Frey could accept all this, but not the almost disgraceful way in which they were refraining from taking him into their confidence.

The coded message had not been signed, but was formulated in such a way that there could be no doubt it was genuine. It had ended with = /, which meant that the future guest and Jonas Mikael Frey were of equal standing, and that neither could compel the other to do anything he did not wish to. It was a confusing paradox. Even if the equals sign was a conciliatory aspect of the laconically worded message, it was not enough to dissipate Frey's discomfort. He had no chance of protesting against being involved in a mission, the nature of which had not been revealed to him but which he could not withdraw from anyway, and hence he was already deeply involved. If it was going too far to say he had been tricked, he had certainly been manipulated.

Frey was used to making up his own mind, and fought against any attempt to put him on a leash. He hated military discipline and despised false submissiveness. The risks he was prepared to take and repeatedly took—they were unavoidable—were conscious ones and a consequence of his own decisions, hence exclusively his own business. If he failed, he could never blame his failure on someone else. He asked nobody for advice and was not above manipulating others, although he did not allow anybody to manipulate him. Once he had made up his mind, he never hesitated to carry his decision through.

Such an attitude might be seen as indicating an over-blown estimate of himself, but that would be a dubious judgment. Frey had good reasons for sticking to his principle of acting like a lone wolf. He was careful to avoid involving others in his decisions for the simple reason that he wanted to have exclusive control over the whole process. He knew the biggest mistake he could make was imparting to others knowledge he was probably alone in possessing.

He seldom discussed methods with his masters. They simply submitted their requests, often in the form of a broad survey of current objectives, a sort of Christmas shopping list, in the hope that one or two of the requests might be fulfilled with the cooperation of Frey. They then drew up an order of preference, but avoided specific demands. They also

13

conducted their mutual financial affairs in an admittedly bureaucratic and occasionally penny-pinching way that was nevertheless quite acceptable. You could say they treated him with respect.

Frey considered himself master of his own house, and until now had always thought he would continue to be that. The flow of information from him and his accomplices was more than satisfactory, and its quality was high. From the point of view of costs, too, his activities were profitable if not extravagantly successful. Millions and millions had been saved thanks to the sophisticated technical information he had acquired and then successfully smuggled over the border. Many of his informers were in key Swedish industries, and there was never any second-rate material in his mail. Whether or not the material was properly exploited by the receiver is another matter. Sometimes, indeed quite often, he had his doubts on that score.

He had two basic working principles. His network of contacts had to remain intact, and it must not be put under strain. At the slightest suggestion of disturbances or risk of exposure, he closed down the whole network. He had agents who had been forced into idleness for five years or more simply because of a careless remark in a board room or from a bar stool.

In between times, he kept reading in the newspapers about raids made by the customs or munitions department on computerized data being smuggled out to the Soviet Union. The reason was nearly always clumsiness or a degree of naïveté that amazed him. These deals were being run by amateurs on both sides. Greed, corruption, and, most of all, a lack of trust were the main reason for these fiascos. The two sides just could not trust each other. It was as simple as that.

Frey did not trust anyone either, but both he and his masters had realized long ago that distrust must be balanced and possibly even replaced by mutual dependence. Generosity in this respect need not mean carelessness or recklessness.

Essential checks can be made without causing bad blood, provided both sides are agreed on the necessity. Checks can be disguised as security measures—the distinction between supervision and protection is hard to define. The effectiveness of a protective system can only be tested when a serious crisis arises—if in an emergency a supervisor cannot be transformed into an energetic guardian and savior, the supervision has been pointless. The savior is never unprepared for the task facing him. All his long, patient wait has been directed at the point when he can make his crucial contribution at the critical moment.

Whatever was in store for Frey, he was convinced that no one was setting a trap for him. The reverse was more likely, and that they wanted to make him more active and more aggressive. He wondered how many dossiers they had ploughed through before settling on his. They would have been looking for someone they could rely on completely and whose loyalty they had no reason to call into question. At the same time, he must have fulfilled one other equally important criterion. He must be sufficiently competent.

Frey was not averse to recognition even though he considered himself immune to flattery. As he stood at his window looking out into the frozen and indifferent winter's night, he could not help smiling to himself. They knew him well in Berlin. The equals sign had not been put there by accident. They knew how to go about ensuring his loyalty while at the same time indirectly and subtly indicating that their confidence in his judgment and ability was undiminished. Was that why they had given him the rare and far-reaching right to impose a veto? A restricted veto, it is true, and only with regard to his own participation, but even so . . . ?

Frey must have allowed his attention to wander, as he was surprised by the doorbell. He had not been alerted by the sound of the elevator machinery and footsteps on the stairs,

15

and was annoyed as he turned away from the window and went to answer the door. He did not bother to put another light on, and left the hall in the dark. A couple of paces short of the outside door, he spun around and went back into the room in order to get rid of his cigarette. He took his time over it, and an ironic smile settled on his lips.

The second ring was much louder, indicating impatience or, possibly, nervousness. Of course, he was being petty, but even if his behavior was childish, it was not unconsidered or psychologically irrelevant. Delaying the meeting for a minute was in a way Frey's revenge for the nine days of enforced idleness spent in his apartment. He wanted to get his own back and, even though it was only for a minute, let the stranger experience the uncertainty and false belief he himself had been forced to live with for far too many days.

Just as Frey was about to take hold of the door handle, a sudden thought struck him and he paused anew. What would he do if he opened the door and found a woman standing there? Although he had had nine whole days to think about it, this was the first time that possibility had entered his head. His ironic smile melted into a sarcastic grin as he unhooked the safety chain and opened the door.

Outside, in the sickly pale light of the landing, was a short man in a dark overcoat cut in continental style and a heavy woolen scarf wrapped around his neck. On his head was a narrow-brimmed hat offering scant protection for his ears, which were blazing red while the color of his cheeks was neutralized by a growth of dark stubble. The man must have been out in the cold for quite some time. He had probably been trying to make sure he was alone and was not being followed. His eyes were brown with a hint of green. As far as Frey could tell, the stranger seemed to be about ten years younger than he was—in other words, around forty.

"Ich bin da," said the man in German with a wry smile, as if to suggest the agreed opening phrase was excessively infantile. In fact, it seemed quite reasonable in his language.

"Come in."

He had just one suitcase.

"The Colonel sends his greetings," said the German once he had taken off his outdoor clothes. "He asked me to give you this."

That same, wry smile again.

For the third time in ten days Frey was given a matchbox with a label depicting a defiant two-tongued dragon.

"I'm starting to get used to them," said Frey.

There was something ridiculous about the whole ritual, and that could well have been the very moment when Frey first detected a relationship between them. They could have been half-brothers. They did not look very much alike, but there was a natural directness about the other man's behavior, a sort of discerning straightforwardness that toned down the dramatic aspects of the meeting between the two agents. They would have no trouble in understanding each other, but it would also make it more difficult to conceal their real intentions. A close relationship does not always entail love and trust, and there is no more dangerous a friend than the one who has managed to penetrate your protective barrier. Only when he has turned into an enemy do you realize how incautious you have been.

"It says in my passport that I'm called Herwart Klammer," said the German.

"That's good enough for me. Have you had a difficult journey?"

"I hadn't expected it to be so cold," replied Klammer.

They went together to the spare room, which led off the living room but also had its own entrance from the landing.

Frey led the way. He was carrying the suitcase, and in the half-light the German was able to study the Swede's back and slightly rounded shoulders from behind. Frey put the light on and paused in the doorway of the simply furnished room. With a slight nod of the head, he invited Klammer to move in and take possession. It was a polite gesture, and if

17

not obsequious then at least respectful. The German stepped past him, and when he turned around after inspecting the room, the wry smile had returned to his face.

"Mr. Frey," he said in a serious tone, without a trace of arrogance or ingratiation. "I might have to stay with you for a whole month. I'll try and be honest with you as far as I can. The Colonel has spelled out for me exactly who and what you are. We don't need to play games with each other."

It was a reprimand.

Frey realized he had underestimated the German, and hence had lost the first round. He gave him a friendly nod even so, and his face betrayed no sign of self-reproach on account of his frivolousness.

"Skepticism is always an advantage in our line of business," said Frey later that night. "First impressions of a person are not always well founded. Even so, I'm convinced already that you and I are going to work well together."

"That was a precondition of our teaming up," said Klammer in a serious voice. "Your contribution is of great importance. As you know, I can't order you to do anything at all."

"We're on an equal footing."

"That's what they say," said Klammer, holding out his hand to seal their relationship with a handshake.

2

When the Russian entered the pressroom and paused in the doorway for a few seconds, the hum of conversation was drowned by the din coming from the exhibition hall. Behind him was a confusion of hissing and whistling, pounding and swishing, and when he eventually got around to closing the door, it was as quiet as a church.

The room was full of men smoking, glasses in hand, and those who had not found anywhere to sit turned away in embarrassment, so that the Russian found himself wandering along a path between hedges of averted faces. He did not seem in the least perturbed. In both build and appearance, he was an insignificant man; but his back was as straight as a ramrod and he moved with a dignity and self-confidence that was not in the least put on. He was formally dressed in a dark suit, and his somber tie indicated lifelong service as a bureaucrat. In his hand was a briefcase almost as big as a suitcase. When he reached the impressive-looking desk at the far end of the room, where the exhibition press officer Gerd Angerbo was holding court, he bowed politely and held out his hand in greeting.

19

"Welcome, Dr. Gusov," said the press officer. "I saw you at the opening ceremony and hoped you would have time to stop by. Did you have a chance to talk to the minister?"

The Russian shook his head despondently, as if the question were out of place or too indiscreet.

"Whiskey? Or maybe you'd rather have a vodka?"

She knew in advance he would decline. When she realized he was in the process of formulating a question in his formal Swedish, she forestalled him by rising to her feet. With an exaggeratedly explicit gesture, she pointed to the row of green-covered collapsible tables lined up along one of the walls, each one piled high with brochures, elegant plastic folders, and endless photographs of machines, tools, and managing directors eager to assist all and sundry in improving their output. All available press releases and advertising handouts were gathered together on the tables.

"It's all there," said the press officer.

A sneering grin spread like wildfire through the room and even rubbed off on Gerd Angerbo, who had difficulty in controlling her amusement. Her proud, mocking gaze swept around the room until it settled once more on the Russian, who seemed unmoved and perhaps also uncomprehending. Despite her efforts, she could not help laughing. It burst from her lips like a shameless seagull's cry.

"Would you like me to give you a hand?" she asked, her guilty conscience getting the better of her as she laid her hand on the Russian's arm.

"No, that's all right, thank you," answered Dr. Gusov. "I can manage quite well by myself."

Dimitri Gusov, doctor of technology and an attaché with the Russian trade delegation in Stockholm, was well known to the assembly of technical journalists. He turned up at all industrial fairs throughout the country, always sat in on the front row during the opening ceremony, alongside colleagues from his own and other embassies, but he was the only one of the VIPs to honor the pressroom with a visit an hour or so later. He always had with him a briefcase the size of a suitcase, and he behaved in exactly the same way every time. He asked permission, which was always granted, to look through the press material and take a copy of anything he found interesting. Nothing had ever been known to be sufficiently lacking in interest for it to escape Dr. Gusov's bulging briefcase.

On once occasion, two journalists had had a bet. They had been discussing Dr. Gusov's technical qualifications. One of them took it for granted that the Russian was a fully qualified engineer and that his title was genuine—why else would they have sent him abroad? The other, a bleary-eyed skeptic, insisted that all Russians allowed to travel abroad were KGB agents, and that Dr. Gusov's technical knowledge was elementary. They agreed to set a trap for the Russian. In amongst the brand-new handouts they slid a well-thumbed brochure advertising an old tool that had ceased production long before, and then they kept a close watch on Dr. Gusov. When he found the brochure featuring the obsolete device, he did not react in the least. He studied it briefly, nodded, and put it in his briefcase without batting an eyelid. The next second, he treated a leaflet for a brand new robot in exactly the same way.

At this point, one of the pair had to acknowledge he had lost his bet. Later on at the bar, however, he expressed his firm conviction that there was still no proof that the Russian was a KGB agent. It would be truer to say he had become even more convinced that Russian technology was still floundering in the stone age. Nevertheless, he was prepared to stand a round of drinks, provided the expense was reasonable.

There was nothing dubious about what Dr. Gusov was doing. On the contrary! It was both desirable and welcome, not only from the point of view of the fair and the exhibitors, but also from that of the nation. Without trade between the two countries, Sweden would be lost—and the trade balance with the Soviet Union showed a regrettable deficit to the tune of several billion kronor. If Russian interest in Swedish goods could be aroused by means of a few brochures, then by all means there was nothing wrong with that.

Gerd Angerbo had another reason for welcoming Dr. Gusov's visit. When the fair was over, she would have to console a lot of disappointed exhibitors with no alternative but to acknowledge that most of the publicity handouts they had assembled with considerable effort and at great expense were still lying there on the tables, untouched.

"The Russians," she could whisper, with a knowing look. "The Russians were very interested indeed in your products. I'd be very surprised if they don't follow it up. But you know how it is, there's such a lot of hemming and hawing before they're ready to make the first move."

No one could accuse her of lying. Russian interest in the mass of brochures and press releases was even greater than the specialist journalists suspected. The previous evening, when all the preparations for the opening ceremony had been made, Gerd Angerbo had just one more little job to do. She was the one who had urged the exhibitors to produce so much publicity material for the press office: There it all was, spread out on the green tables, the raw material for the give away file she had prepared for all the journalists. Late that night she had taken a copy of every brochure, sketch, photograph, technical or financial description, and locked the bulky collection away in a cupboard. Eventually it would be picked up by someone from the Soviet embassy. It seemed as if the Russian trade delegation was either unaware of what their diplomatic colleagues were up to, or preferred to ignore them. Gerd had often wondered whether Dr. Gusov knew he was competing with his own countrymen.

A readiness to help and cooperate deserves acknowledgment. The Russians expect to be coolly received in the West, and there is always a danger they might overreact to unexpected benevolence. The previous Christmas, Gerd was

22

delighted to note that she was evidently more appreciated by the Russian Trade Delegation than by the embassy. Dr. Gusov himself had presented her with a case of whiskey, while the embassy had merely sent round a driver with a bottle of vodka.

Frey had happened to see the case of whiskey when he paid her one of his rare visits shortly after the New Year and somewhat cheekily peered into her pantry. It was immediately obvious that the bottles had not been processed by Swedish customs.

"What's all this? Don't tell me you've started smuggling?" he asked her.

"Of course not," she said with a laugh.

"It's a Christmas Box." She added after a little hesitation, "From the Russian embassy."

If Frey had been a little more wide awake, he would have noticed that her voice had broken into a falsetto. It tended to do that when she was under pressure. But her reply made him surprised rather than suspicious. They very size of the present suggested the recipient was a particularly useful contact.

"Do you get lots of presents like this?" he asked.

"No," she said, her voice normal again now. "The embassy was just thanking me for my contribution to last year's technology jamboree when the Soviet Union had a pretty big stand. I did what I could to help, and by God, it was an effort. I wouldn't be surprised if I spent half my time on them. You don't think this present has anything to do with our little business, do you?"

Frey shook his head.

"Of course not," he said, and meant it. "Only I and possibly your own contacts know of your existence in this context. There's no dossier on you, not even a speculative one. You can feel quite safe. Regard these gifts as proof of how competent and professional you are, my dear press officer."

They sampled the whiskey and proposed a toast to their mutual welfare. Gerd tried to steer the conversation into new pastures, but Frey kept coming back to the Russians' astonishing generosity.

"If anybody from the embassy starts displaying unusual interest in you and your activities, you must let me know immediately," he said, pensively. "Especially if they go on about extending your cooperation. We don't want any bulls in our china shop."

"Meaning?"

"Meaning nothing at all."

He smiled that broad smile of his, the smile she found so hard to resist, the one he had found so useful in recruiting her once upon a time, several summers ago.

"The risk is minimal, to say the least," he went on, not unmoved. "The delegation here in Stockholm no doubt assume your links with SÄPO are intimate. Any other state of affairs would be unthinkable in Moscow or New York. In a modest way, I suppose I've encouraged them to form that opinion."

When he saw how astonished she looked, he couldn't help roaring with laughter.

"What have you done?" she asked. She sounded really angry.

"I've just put out a safety net," he replied calmly. "That's something we could all do with."

Her immediate reaction was to shake her head, but then her eyes started to gleam.

"You swine," she said.

She was like a chameleon. Just now, her smile was so warm, so jolly, so tempting, that anybody, apart from those who knew her well, would have to assume it was genuine. That was why he had picked her. Her wide range of contacts and her central position with regard to Swedish industry were not enough in themselves. Nor were her monumental egoism or her need to assert herself. If she hadn't been so

24

good at dissimulating, he would never have been able to trust her. She was a great actress, there was no part she could not play; and he had always suspected she had no soul.

"Have you lots of secrets you don't tell me?" she asked, ingratiatingly.

"None at all. And you?"

"Of course not. You're like a confessor to me."

It sounded like a lie, but he let it pass as the truth.

The pressroom had started to empty. Among the noisy machines in the hall downstairs, exhibitors were lying in wait, desperate for publicity. In practically every pavilion and most of the bigger stands was a bar cupboard that opened immediately on sight of a press card. That blessed insignia of office seemed to radiate "Open Sesame" here at the fair.

Only the Russian, Dr. Gusov, carried on as before, indefatigably collecting his leaflets.

When the door from the exhibition hall opened again, Gerd Angerbo knew she would be relieved at last: dealing with the journalists was becoming more and more trying as time went by. The newcomer paused briefly to greet Dr. Gusov, who was forced to break off in order to shake hands and mutter a few polite phrases.

The new arrival was a man in the prime of his life, still in his thirties. He was elegantly dressed, as one might expect of a press secretary from a ministry on official business. His blond hair had been ruffled by the drafts down in the exhibition hall, emphasizing the boyish nervousness of his behavior. Alf Skolle was a good-looking fellow, convinced he knew how best to make the most of his charm.

"Sorry I'm late," he said, ignoring the three journalists still sitting in front of Gerd Angerbo. "My boss insisted I should go with him to see the Rumanians—you know how he's dying to develop more trade with the Eastern bloc. We've been invited to Bucharest, in fact. Not formally, of course. That kind of invitation usually goes through the Foreign

Office. But they proposed a toast in that awful plum brandy they insist on offering everybody, and said they were looking forward to seeing us in Rumania in the near future."

He smiled broadly at everyone as if he had just revealed a sensational piece of news.

"They'd better get a move on then," boomed a hoarse voice. It came from a giant of a man whose enormous belly was threatening to bend the arms of the chair he had forced himself into.

"What do you mean?" asked Skolle, his voice suddenly betraying traces of venom and suspicion.

The colossus grinned. "I just meant they'd better get the visit over by summer at the latest. There's an election this autumn, and who knows? It might be somebody else that gets the free trip to Bucharest."

Skolle ignored the rude remark. He had built up his career in the labor movement, in what had become the orthodox progression of university, committees, and elegant dinners. There was nothing proletarian about him. Although he had spent several years working for working-class news-papers, he had never adopted the slangy colloquial language that distinguished journalists from better-bred citizens. Skolle was a stickler for etiquette, and he never missed an opportunity of letting those with whom he came into contact know that he walked the corridors of power.

Pursing his lips, he turned to Gerd Angerbo.

"Are you ready?" he asked.

She nodded and rose to her feet.

"I'll be back in an hour," she announced, treating all present to her winning smile. "Irma will look after you till then."

She paused in the doorway and turned to face the room.

"Good-bye, Dr. Gusov," she said in a loud voice. "Why don't you call back when we've both got a bit more time?"

The Russian broke of in the middle of collecting another brochure. When he bowed in acknowledgment, he looked as if he were standing to attention. If anyone had bothered to observe him a little more closely—but why should they?—they might have noticed an amused glint in those eyes of his that always seemed so melancholy. Although no one present would have thought it, not even for a moment, Dr. Gusov did in fact have a sense of humor, and often smiled—indeed, he frequently laughed, even if he was perverse enough to do so when he was all alone, generally speaking.

Gerd Angerbo had a table reserved exclusively for her own use in the smaller of the restaurants at the exhibition center. The lighting there was more discreet, and there was a better chance of being able to conduct a private conversation without being disturbed or overheard than in the main restaurant, where the tables were much closer together, and you could never be sure who would be sitting next to you.

She had ordered drinks, and when they toasted each other, she noticed that Alf Skolle's hand was shaking, so much so that he spilled a few drops on the tablecloth.

"You look tired," she said, sympathetically. "Is he pestering you with too much work, as usual?"

"He can be very trying," admitted the press secretary, "but then, all ministers are the same. On the other hand, he still makes me very much into his confidence. Maybe you know we were both chairman of the same Young Socialists group. Admittedly, there were fifteen years between us, but even so."

"That's the kind of thing that binds people together," remarked Gerd with a smile.

"So they say."

Despite his youth, his elegant attire, and his man-of-the-world attitude, the man facing Gerd Angerbo looked not only tired, but tense. He was blinking more frequently than normal, and his bright, blue eyes under those thick, bushy eyebrows of his seemed watery and hesitant. On closer inspection, she realized they were also bloodshot and gathered he had started drinking.

"I've got a present for you," she said, handing him one of the portfolios of press handouts.

He looked at her inquiringly.

"The contents are strictly personal," she went on, her tone evasive and not without irony. "I'd say they were worth six thousand kronor. You'll find them in the inside pocket."

He reached out for the portfolio, eager to get hold of the money, but she grasped his arm immediately.

"Not now," she whispered, and it sounded just like the hiss of a viper. "Wait until you're on your own."

He jerked back in his chair like a schoolboy caught in the act. Then his expression changed, his eyes filled with cunning as he jutted out his chin. He looked evil.

"Presents demand presents in return," he said teasingly. "Here's the minister's inaugural speech. Pages four to six are especially interesting."

She had no choice but to take the speech. The money in the batch of press handouts was not incriminating; the minister's speech, however, did not in fact contain the original words on the pages referred to, but a summary of the minimal conditions established by the Swedish government a few days previously with regard to the forthcoming negotiations with the People's Republic of Poland for an extension of their credit terms, and possibly an increase. The document had immediately been classified Top Secret. Apart from the minister and the man responsible for negotiations between the two countries, Alf Skolle was the only one in the ministry who knew exactly what it said. In a few days' time the contents would also be known to a small group of people in Warsaw.

Just as he had expected, she was absolutely furious and for the rest of the meal replied to his questions offhandedly and in monosyllables. Skolle had managed to restore a little of his former self-confidence.

He ordered a double brandy with his coffee, and observed how she thought of checking him. When she pursed her lips and said nothing, he began to feel quite pleased with himself. He had put her in her place. About time, too.

Then she startled him by calling the waiter back and ordering a liqueur.

"This really is going a bit far," she said, pouting. "We have to be careful. Both of us."

He nodded, and grinned cheekily at her.

"You're a pest," she said.

"Always happy to oblige," he replied.

Dr. Gusov was all alone at one of the smaller tables, contemplating his steak, a beer, and a large vodka. As the information officer and press secretary walked past him, Skolle nodded in greeting. Gerd was immediately behind him, so he did not see the friendly nod she received as she passed the Russian's table, studiously stroking the handbag in which she had put the minister's inaugural address.

For once, it looked as if Dr. Gusov was actually smiling in public.

3

Jonas Mikael Frey was aware that he had been humiliated, but he also acknowledged it was largely his own fault. He had been put in his place without a single word being uttered, or a gesture made.

Most humiliations are self-induced and, as in Frey's case, due to underestimating someone, or failing to see far enough ahead. Getting over a serious personal insult requires both strength and humility. Gifted people usually turn to irony, and anyone able to laugh at himself is regarded rightly or wrongly as a strong character.

That is easily said. For someone whose only resource is his strictly limited and, even in his own eyes, monotonously boring life, every humiliation, whether or not it is self-inflicted, is a slap in the face, and the only possible reaction is fury. An insult opens up painful wounds in one's self-confidence, and most people have no alternative but to slink away and lick their wounds. Our ability to forget, to suppress all memories, is a great healer, and the scar usually mends surprisingly quickly, without our even noticing that our self-respect has shrunk and can never again be taken for granted or be as great as it once was.

It does occasionally happen that a wound of that sort has difficulty in healing, and leaves an ugly scar as a constant reminder of the insult. People like that are made in such a way that the thought of revenge easily takes root, and keeps on growing stronger and stronger until there is no alternative but to turn the thought into action.

For a secret agent, who has to spend his whole life constantly trying to control every action and cannot allow himself the luxury of a single emotionally overcharged reaction, humiliation can be turned to his own advantage.

Although Frey was still smarting, he had lost neither his self-control nor his judgment. Despite the bitterly cold winter, he had been stung by a wasp, and the sting was still itching painfully. In an hour or two it would have gone, and the only trace of it in his memory would be in the form of a warning and a challenge. Watch out! Don't underestimate him! There's no way in which he's inferior to you.

Really, nothing at all had happened.

Suddenly and without warning, Herwart Klammer had come to a halt outside a dance restaurant tempting the passerby with music, warmth, red tablecloths, and fir twigs in the windows. As luck would have it, Frey was halfway between two doorways and did not manage to make the tobacconist's before Klammer's gaze turned in his direction. Klammer had the wind behind him just at that point, and although he was over fifty yards away and Frey could barely make out the German, he was convinced he had been spotted.

A series of snow flurries had drifted in from Finland and were whirling their way down Västerlånggatan in the Old Town. A few pedestrians in fur coats were struggling along against the wind, their heads bowed and tears streaming from their eyes. Step by step, their eyes glued stubbornly to a spot on the slippery pavement barely a shoe's length in front of their toes, they pressed on, cursing the moment they had been forced to leave their nice, warm homes.

Those lucky enough to have the wind behind them, on the other hand, were having to dig in their heels in order to slow down and keep control of themselves. Half running, their chins in the air, they strove to steer their way down the street with the fixed stare familiar on drivers careering along a motorway. For anyone with the wind behind him, the view ahead was quite good despite the dancing snow. A simple fact of life that Frey had failed to take into account. A sin of omission, yes indeed, but one sufficiently minor as to give hope of absolution.

Frey had been shadowing Klammer for half an hour. He had seen the German buy a newspaper and a picture postcard at one of the stalls in the Central Station, and he watched him post the card in the mailbox in the middle of the forecourt. Then he had followed him over the Riksbron Bridge and into Västerlånggatan. Kept an eye on him, would perhaps be more accurate. Made sure no unauthorized person was following him. Ensured the safety of Herwart Klammer, and thus complied with his instructions. There were plenty of excuses for what he had done.

Nevertheless, none of them was valid for the simple reason that Klammer had made it clear he wanted to be on his own the first few days in Stockholm, and did not need protecting. Although they had agreed to operate on their own for the time being, the German had obviously expected Frey to be following him. He had let it go on for half an hour before signaling that enough was enough.

Frey had to admit that Klammer had not made a fuss, and there was no way he had been provocative or demonstrative. But the message was clear and unmistakable. That's enough. Thus far and no farther. I know you're there, and I don't like it.

The really humiliating part of it was that Klammer had so easily given the thumbs-down to Frey's ability to trail him without being discovered, and that he had let it go on for so long without putting a stop to it.

Klammer had not suggested Frey was an amateur, he had not even snubbed him; all he had done was to signal gently that he wanted to be left alone. They had not said a word, just looked long and hard at each other. That was enough.

The girl in the tobacconist's was glad of the break. The afternoon had been just one long yawn, and the few customers she had served were as frosty in their demeanor as in their appearance. This tall man had a pleasant smile and a friendly look in his eye. He seemed to be in no hurry, and had time for a chat. She took an instant liking to him.

Frey had always found it easy to dissemble. Just now, his friendliness and small talk was his way of letting off steam. He needed to reduce the tension inside him and recover his equilibrium. Deep down, he was furious; but he did not show it. He was furious with Klammer, who had humiliated him; with the Colonel and all the rest of them who had placed him in such an idiotic situation; with the awful weather, but most of all with himself.

There was nothing Frey disliked more than failure, and he had good grounds for his dislike of it. As far as he was concerned, failure nearly always meant exposing himself to extreme danger. He had been careless and light-headed, and recognition of this fact must not be allowed to prevent him from getting a grip on himself. He must swallow his annoyance and try to turn what had happened to his own advantage.

Frey was a model of politeness and good manners as he took his leave of the girl in the shop, but the moment he closed the door behind him the smile faded from his lips. He looked calm and resolute once more. An observer would have judged him to be a dangerous man, and in no way did he seem to be beaten.

As he emerged into the street he bumped into a stocky little man muffled up to the eyeballs, his close-fitting woolen hat merely serving to emphasize the rotundity of his head. The stranger took a step backward and allowed Frey to pass, his childlike smile lighting up the whole of his face. Frey barely noticed his presence. He was far too busy thinking about other things, and it would be some minutes before he settled down and took in what was happening around him.

All morning, Jonas Mikael Frey and Herwart Klammer had been sitting at the kitchen table like two hardened poker players getting to know each other's game before getting down to serious business. Both of them were equally good at handling the cards. The stakes were low, and when either of them demanded to see, nothing but small fry were laid out on the table. Their manner was unfailingly polite, and they bartered small talk while being careful to avoid pressuring their opponent. In many respects, their breakfast-time conversation was reminiscent of an East German party delegation meeting their Swedish equivalents: everything friendly and intimate on the surface, but no one was quite sure who mistrusted whom most.

It was only when they started to discuss practical details that their conversation became more relaxed, though one could hardly describe it as being intimate.

They had gone down together in the elevator to the basement of the apartment block.

"The laundry room is shared by all the tenants on all three staircases," Frey explained. "This means that if you use this door, you can get to and from my apartment via any of the entrances. The risk of bumping into any of the neighbors is negligible. In the evening, at any rate."

"Excellent," said Klammer. "If you think it's advisable, I'll use different entrances in turn."

Frey nodded.

"On the other hand," he went on, "it's very easy to keep an eye on all three entrances from the other side of the street, and so I've fixed myself an emergency exit."

"Interesting."

"This key marked in red," explained Frey, holding up a bunch of keys, "opens that door in front of us. That's my emergency exit. The grocer has his storeroom in there, and there's a loading bay and ramp from the back of the building. It takes fifteen seconds at most to pass through the storeroom. The door to the ramp opens from the inside, and once you're through there, you're in the rear courtyard.

"Splendid."

"If I were you, I'd have a scout around. If you can get out into the rear courtyard, you'll be surprised how many options you have."

Klammer took the keys and smiled in appreciation.

"You're a man who plans ahead, Mr. Frey," he said. "Not that I'm surprised—they made it clear in Berlin you are a competent professional."

"Making sure you have a way of retreat is pretty elementary, don't you think?"

"Of course."

Klammer drew himself up to his full height and swallowed a couple of times, as if searching for the right words.

"I am convinced, my dear comrade," he said at last. "No, I'm absolutely certain that I'll never need to use this key. I don't intend attracting any undue attention to myself. As you will have noticed, I shan't take advantage of your undoubted skill and experience unless I really have to. Most probably, I shan't need your assistance until the very end of my stay here in Stockholm. To tell you the truth, I hope I'll be able to take leave of you without having caused you any notable inconvenience other than the necessity of putting up with an uninvited guest in your apartment for a few weeks."

"I'm at your service," replied Frey.

They took the elevator back to the apartment, and stood contemplating each other in the mirror. Klammer was smiling.

"Don't let my visit interfere with your plans, at least not for the next ten days or so," he said benevolently. "I can manage quite well on my own."

"I've been made responsible for your safety," responded Frey.

Klammer laughed.

"Yes, of course," he said, "but the only danger I shall be exposed to in the immediate future is the possibility of being hit on the head by a lump of ice from some roof or other. Not even you can protect me from that."

If Herwart Klammer had been more communicative, it is possible that Frey would have told him about a fifth way of getting out of the building, the best of them all. It was known only to himself and a few construction workers on the underground who had moved on some time ago.

Quite recently, a new extension of the Stockholm underground had been opened, and one of the newly built stations was back-to-back with the apartment block where Frey lived. In connection with the construction work, the underground people had rented some unused storage space in Frey's basement. The workers had destroyed the outside wall but left the original door into the basement corridor. A newly installed safety lock, difficult to force, was intended to deter tenants from using this shortcut into the station.

With the aid of an unscrupulous and anarchistically inclined Austrian who traveled all over the world building underground railways and making use of his expertise in locks, Frey had go hold of the relevant keys. The Austrian had a highly developed sense of humor and was delighted at the thought of his newly acquired Swedish friend being able

36

to slip into the underground whenever he liked, without paying. A generous supply of schnapps and Bavarian beer had facilitated the negotiations, which had not been all that difficult in any case. They were conducted by Frey in perfect German.

4

Even if the telephone conversation had been tapped, which was unlikely, an eavesdropper would have had difficulty in making any sense out of the confused exchanges.

It sounded just like any other wrong-number call: mutual irritation and disappointment, misunderstandings, and, eventually, a few meaningless words of apology.

The woman who answered did not betray any hint of surprise, despite the fact that she must have recognized his voice. Afterward she wondered whether his tired, lifeless tone was put on or not. She knew he had his periods of depression—they could last for weeks—and it was after all several months since they had last seen each other. They did not talk about the depressions she used to have in the past. When she was with him, she never displayed any melancholy.

Generally speaking, Frey avoided the telephone. It is a treacherous device and has caught out many an unsuspecting risk-taker. The mere fact of ringing a number can be enough to alert the security forces. Frey therefore always assumed his own telephone conversations might be recorded. He only used his home telephone in connection with his work as a free-lance journalist, and if he needed to make some really important or unavoidable call, he would take the car to Uppsala or Väteraås and look for a phone booth that had not been vandalized. His name and number were in the directory. For the people he was up against, it was just as easy to find out about ex-directory numbers as it was for a postman to read a nameplate on a door.

If there was a noticeable increase in the number of wrong-number calls he received at home (more than one every other month), he was on the alert and assumed that either he was being watched, or someone was trying to find out whether he was around. A wrong-number call is a quick, cheap, and simple way of checking a person's whereabouts, and for that very reason, it is perhaps not completely reliable or risk-free. For a secret agent, any variation in the dull, everyday routine, no matter how innocent it may seem, is a clear signal to be on one's guard. The same applies to the professional eavesdropper. Like the agent, he has chosen to live with suspicion as his constant bedfellow.

After making a mess of his attempt at shadowing, Frey had withdrawn to a bar in order to restore his confidence and sense of proportion. He thought the matter over and concluded he needed help. He had a built-in reluctance to involve anyone else in his business, but although this was an admirable principle, he had to admit there was some merit in the theory that a rule is only applicable if it allows exceptions.

He had half a dozen names to choose from, and went through them all carefully. It was an unnecessarily complicated procedure, and was really an excuse to while away a few hours—he had made up his mind even before he started to go through the list. Even so, he examined the other five very carefully. Perhaps he was half-hoping he could find some way of not dragging her into this diffuse business; he had no way of gauging the risks or the implications at this stage.

He could rely on her absolutely—that applied to all of them. But none of the others could match her when it came to qualifications for the job he had in mind. Moreover, he would never need to lie to her, because she never asked unnecessary questions. She was neither unsuspecting nor dependent on others, but even so, she was unswervingly loyal, especially to him.

Meanwhile, he wondered how much she really meant to him, and how much he meant to her. He had always avoided answering that question, probably due to cowardice.

In their relationship, and that is what it was in spite of everything, there was a tacit holding back. They would not allow themselves to get too close. They were very similar in many respects. Both of them had scars and burns. Both had been through painful experiences of their own but had managed to pull through, often in similar fashion. Nevertheless, they were different in several vital ways. Not just because one of them was a man and the other a woman, but because Frey was basically a restless person who avoided looking over his shoulder whenever possible, and hence had his gaze fixed firmly before him; she, on the other hand, longed for the peace and harmony that can only be attained if there is a living bond between the present and the past.

Marriage between them would have been no better or worse than any other marriage. As time went by, they would have drawn back into their shells and reduced each other to pale shadows of their former selves. Like many another couple, they would have sat silently in each other's company. They had too much to hide, and both of them knew that lighthearted frankness even between themselves could only lead to ruin. In the end, they would have had just one shared conviction: the acknowledgment that it had all been meaningless.

Frey sought protection behind this bitter conclusion,

knowing that it was only an excuse to avoid making up his mind. He was ready to run away at any moment, and only when it was too late had he begun to realize that his constant readiness to flee led him into a state of incurable isolation. He had given up companionship for isolation, which meant security as far as he was concerned. He had put loyalty before love, which he was afraid of because it encouraged one to indulge in self-assertion, frivolity, and exaggeration. He had chosen to place limitations on his life, and it was poor consolation for him that other people's lives seemed to be at least as limited.

He had kept away from her for an unusually long time, and he suspected he might have hurt her, that she imagined he had left her out in the cold because he considered her inadequate. That was a painful and unjust accusation. He quickly made up an acceptable explanation, an excuse, despite the fact that it contained a contradiction. He told himself he had kept away because he cared about her, it was a matter of solicitude, possibly even love. He wanted to protect her from unhappiness, the insidious unhappiness he always brought along with him and which others—not he—could turn into harsh reality.

Nevertheless, he did not hesitate for a moment to visit her that evening and take her into his confidence—despite the obvious risks. It was a paradoxical decision, not least because he felt no guilt in making it.

Frey was still fumbling in the dark. The threat was there, but it was vague and intangible. He had been given a role in a play, but he had no script and did not know who the director was. He was now going to add a secondary character to the cast, and in doing so, make the outcome more difficult for the producer to forecast. Especially as the new role was to be an invisible one and with luck would be undetected to the very end.

The Colonel, spy-master and casting director, stage manager and lighting technician, could hardly condemn such a

41

move. Right at the beginning, he had issued Frey a warning but had also given him a free hand. Just one signal. One that he could well have misinterpreted. People who give signals have always tried to obscure their warnings and predictions behind an impenetrable haze. Once the story is over and the simple plot is clear to everyone, only the signaler can rub his hands together and boast of how he knew it would be like that all the time.

For some time yet the threat would remain vague and indistinct, then it would explode like a bomb. There was not much more he could tell her. Nothing concrete. Just premonitions and suspicions.

A long time ago, quite independently and without pressure from anyone else, but partly due to youthful innocence, both of them had sworn an allegiance that committed them to lifelong loyalty, and which would not allow them to renounce or deviate from it.

She had taken sides in the current worldwide conflict between the rich and the poor, between those who died of starvation and those who died of excess, and she had identified herself completely with the poor. She was very young at the time. She realized later that the real struggle was between the oppressed and the oppressors, between the untrammeled wielders of power and their downtrodden slaves. That struggle was going on all over the world, in the east and west, north and south; in dictatorships, democracies, and religious oligarchies. There was a full spectrum of the misuse of power, ranging from brutal violence to sophisticated control; but the aim was always the same: clinging on to the power a minority had managed to acquire. She had been forced to make the painful discovery that outrages were neither less frequent nor less barbaric on her side than on the other. Even so, she never entertained the idea of breaking the vow she had made. While things seemed to be becoming

42

grimmer in the West, she sometimes thought she could detect a glimmer of hope in the East.

Frey had known her for over ten years, having been given her as a present. That is how the Colonel had put it. She had just turned thirty and was starting to get over the aftermath of a childhood and youth cluttered with outrage, degradation, and humiliation. At an early age she had been encumbered with foster parents who never ceased reminding her how grateful she should be for the cast-off clothing the forced her to wear. She had stubbornly refused to cooperate with competent but indifferent social workers whose casual pats on the back and mean smiles had haunted her in her sleep. She had drifted from classroom to classroom, always picked on by her schoolmates and ignored by her teachers. Wherever she went, she was rejected. No one saw she had remarkable inner strength and unusual intelligence. That is why they did not realize she was concealing behind a mask of embarrassed indifference her boundless contempt for the people who hid their contempt for her.

She eventually went to work and acquired a home of her own, but she could never shake off the label of pariah. As an eighteen-year-old she turned to the Party, and for the first time—it seemed like living proof of the heinous nature of class-ridden society—she was treated on almost equal terms with everyone else. She joined a youth group and found that working-class girls were in a minority. Most of them were well educated and destined for academic careers, and they treated her with the extreme tact that generally conceals either contempt or fear. She had no close friends, but what was more important was that no one attempted to exploit her. She was not called upon to perform the servile duties she was so experienced in, and they spared her the crude coldness of manner with which she had always been treated.

Perhaps it was her undeniable proletarian background which assured her a place in the Swedish youth delegation that spent a summer on the island of Rügen. For the first time her background and experiences were the cause of unfeigned respect, and her hosts soon discovered her considerable talents and potential usefulness. Before long they were offering her education, and then even money. She accepted everything that came her way, and her gratitude was genuine and eternal. They had transformed her from a nobody into a somebody.

Now, at the age of forty, she was a fully-grown, mature woman who had no need to bow her head before anyone.

Her name was Gudrun Brunhildson, and there is no prouder name a woman could bear.

"You want something from me," she said.

"Of course. Why else would I have come?"

Her gaze was curious, and she was summing him up, as if trying to find out straightaway whether he had changed. Her expression was serious. A strand of blond hair hung down over her brow, hiding the furrows. There was something timeless about her, something inscrutably experienced that had nothing at all to do with her age. A superficial observer might find her insignificant, at first glance, partly because she was short in stature but mainly because she was so reserved, almost timid. Her apparently indolent calm was a front to conceal her intelligence, watchfulness, and decisiveness. Frey knew very few people who could match her. She was cunning and brave, but what he admired most was her uncanny ability to make herself invisible.

Suddenly her eyes lit up. She had made an effort to look her best, for his sake, and there was something puckish about her when she eyed him up and down curiously, for the second time. Her expression changed and she suddenly seemed younger as she broke into a smile and the thin little wrinkles around her mouth shifted to form a laugh-line.

"No. Why else would you have come?"

She had prepared herself well, as if she were going to a party. There was a bottle of wine on the table, and a salad.

44

She knew his preference for whiskey. He wouldn't have been surprised if she always had a bottle waiting for him. They drank a toast, and there was no trace of unrest in her eyes, rather a sort of girlish mischief. She oozed that spirited self-confidence women sometimes display when they know that frivolity will soon be replaced by seriousness.

"Gudrun . . ."

She interrupted him.

"I've called in sick," she said. "I'm entirely at your disposal. Day and night."

Frey grunted.

"You don't suppose I've come here just for your sake?" he asked.

"Of course not," she replied. "It's only in my dreams you ring me up and want nothing but me."

Just for a moment, he looked ready to start a quarrel, and she couldn't help laughing out loud.

"You look too ridiculous," she said.

"It's just that you can see through me," he muttered. "Everyone in this comedy is ridiculous. Even you. We jump around the moment anybody pulls our strings, and we appear on the stage for a few moments without anyone noticing we're there. Unlike real actors and all those on the directing side and the stage and the stage designers and the people who always hog the main parts, we never get any applause. They think they know we're there, but nobody ever manages to notice us."

"As long as we don't trip over the footlights or forget our dance steps."

"If we did, they'd chop our heads off," he rejoined sullenly. "But first they'd turn on the spotlights and stick us in the stocks so that everybody could spit at us. Then they'd execute us. As you know, that would be a cleaning up job, and we live in a world that can't stand uncleanliness. Or shit, which is what we are."

"You sound bitter," she said.

45

"Not in the least. I'm just being honest. Comedians like you and me mustn't close our eyes to reality. That's why our eyes look so big and innocent. We see and understand almost everything. In the long run we have to admit that the world is run on the basis of lies and dissimulation, and nobody wants to know the plain unadorned truth."

"People standing in the shadows see more than people in the blinding sunlight."

"That's very true. Maybe we don't let our imaginations run away with us as much as other people do. Unlike them, we've learned to mistrust the great actors. We can see through their big words and grin at their gestures, no matter if they're grandiose or popular. We have nothing but contempt for their empty phrases that attempt to cover up their broken promises, and we know they're all corrupt, all of them, without exception. We've even learned to mistrust our friends, especially when their kindness and consideration starts getting too trying."

"I don't mistrust you."

"But you keep your eye on me. You scrutinize me and listen to my tone of voice and you know straightaway if I'm trying to pull the wool over your eyes. Quite right, too."

She smiled, as if he had just paid her a compliment.

"What do you want me to do?"

He paused for a few seconds before answering, so she would see he was being completely frank.

"I want you to make yourself invisible and become my eyes," he said. "A man has arrived in Stockholm from the Republic. He's staying in my apartment. He's very reticent, far too reticent. I've been warned about him, in a way. I want you to find out who he is, whom he meets, and what he's up to when he's not asleep in my spare bed. Above all, I want to know why he's come here, and what he's intending to do."

"Since when have we been spying on our own side?"

"We've always done that. Paranoia and self-effacement

46

are two irreconcilable qualities, but they are the basis of our activities."

"That sounds unwarranted," she said in astonishment. "Are you suggesting this man's activities are directed against us? Does he belong to the other side?"

"Probably not."

"Then I don't know what you're going on about."

"I haven't got much idea either," Frey said, sighing. "I know next to nothing. Just that he's dangerous, and that he represents a threat."

"To you?"

"Let's assume that," he said. "For the time being, at least."

She noted the irony in his voice, and realized he was as unsure as he sounded. He did not need to explain. She knew all suspicions are fleeting and vague when they are born. Most people try to hold them at arm's length. Any hint of a change affecting the way we live our lives due to the actions or intentions of somebody else, hitherto unnoticed and still barely visible, is a threat to our existence. We prefer to close our eyes and simultaneously start looking around for some more tangible and unequivocal proof. That first fleeting glimpse of danger or treachery becomes a voice nagging away inside. It can be overruled, sure, but never completely eliminated.

A secret agent must be receptive to every hint of a suspicion, no matter how slender. He must react to every false tone of voice, recoil from every unusual meeting, and see through all pretense of innocence. As far as he is concerned, there is always an ulterior motive behind every human action. It does not necessarily follow that their real intention is aimed at him, but he must assume that it might be.

"Does the Colonel know him?" asked Gudrun.

"He's the one who's sent him here."

She looked surprised, almost dismayed.

"And me . . . ?"

Frey shook his head.

"No," he said. "The Colonel's orders are very cryptic on this occasion. He seems to be trying to muzzle me, and yet, at the same time, giving me a free hand. I don't even know how he would react if he knew about our conversation."

She thought for a moment, and he suddenly fell madly in love with the little furrows on her brow, just under her hairline. Then her cheeks filled out, she looked happy, and immediately seemed to be ten years younger.

"In that case," she said with a little smile, "we'd better leave the Colonel out of it. Between comedians like you and me."

There are moments when the stars hide themselves away, as if eternity were taking a rest. Gudrun Brunhildson had crept out of the bed in which Jonas Mikael Frey was still asleep, like a harmless brown bear that had just eaten his fill of sweet honey. She sat in the kitchen, gazing out into the frozen winter's night, at the pitch-black sky arching over the earth like an unsmiling apology. Smiling contentedly, she had slumped down on one of the kitchen chairs and took an occasional sip from a glass of whiskey. She felt liberated and at peace with the world.

Her listlessness had faded away; her melancholy dispersed. In a few hours she would step out into reality— ruthless, terrifying but very real reality. She knew it would show no mercy, and that she must be on her guard. She would slip into it through a secret door, and she hoped no one would notice her arriving or leaving again as she crept back to her hiding place.

As a child, she had learned how to peep unobserved into drawing rooms and bedrooms, and to hide away in bushes or ditches. She had always been used to listening to what other people said, but mainly to their whispers rather than their noisy, self-assured boasts. She had thus obtained insight into

48

all kinds of things that were intended to be secret. Ever since she was a child, she had been skilled at penetrating beyond the carefully made-up and tended mask all upper-class people wear. She had learned to recognize signs of greed and betrayal, selfishness, self-importance and indifference, fear and brutality. Most people who thought they were something had never even noticed her. She was much too insignificant to be taken seriously. Perhaps that was why she saw more than other people, saw through them all, saw things they did not want her to see, and which they never realized she had seen.

An invisible eye. That was how he had put it. She smiled. Somewhat indulgently, as it was an exaggeration; but she was vain enough to feel flattered. Like all really able people, she was only moderately impressed by her own ability. She was well aware of the snags, and knew that chance, which held arbitrary sway over the unforeseen and developments that are only conceivable with hindsight, could unmask her at any moment, making her visible and worthless.

The odds were in her favor. Unlike the stranger, she knew her city inside out and could exploit every opportunity if offered. She could change her appearance and her role whenever she pleased. Her network of contacts among the humble and unnoticed was wide.

If a woman possesses the special skills necessary for a shadowing operation, she is usually preferable to a man. This is especially true during the day and the early evening: different circumstances apply later. Night is the province of the male hunter, and wherever a woman appears on her own, whether it be in a restaurant or a bar, in a dance hall or on the street, she is fair game in the small hours. A woman who reacts differently from the norm (letting herself be picked up, or running away) always runs the risk of attracting attention to herself. Anyone who wants to remain invisible must never attract attention, or even be noticed. The person being followed must never become suspicious, no matter how wary he is.

She was well aware of the terms. Frey was not asking her to find conclusive proof. Her task was to gather pieces of the jigsaw, and it did not matter if a few were missing. Once the pattern began to emerge, he would fill in the gaps for himself. Then, and only then, everything would be over and done with—for this time. She knew that she only had him on loan, as always.

She drew her dressing gown more tightly around her body, as if the cold air outside the kitchen window had crept a little closer. Nothing was going to change. Nothing significant. Nevertheless, she would not change the job she had taken on that evening for anything in the world. It was not the excitement. She hardly ever felt excited. It was not only for his sake either, despite the fact that she was prepared to do almost anything for him. The pleasure she felt went deeper than that. She did not try to explain it. Instead she just sat there, enjoying the misleadingly voluptuous feeling of being able to go out into the world once more in search of revenge.

~5

The brightly decorated exhibition hall was beginning to look shabby. The exquisite floral decorations had started to droop long ago, bombarded by low-flying clouds of cigarette smoke and ambushed by waves of alcoholic haze. As it was the middle of winter, the flowers had been flown in to Stockholm from Holland at ridiculously high cost, but the exhibition manager did not need to fear a reprimand from his board or his accountants. They had all turned up, accompanied by their elegantly dressed and obviously enchanted wives. They mixed with their guests and handled them tactfully on the whole, but occasionally with a trace of condescension. Here as everywhere else there were invisible class barriers, despite the fact that everyone thought they belonged to the establishment. No matter what, there is a difference between an ambassador or minister and a provincial businessman who manufactures roof trusses, or a contractor who runs an office-cleaning firm, even if he does happen to be a boss.

The two staff photographers followed closely on the heels of the VIPs, the blinking of their flashbulbs betraying

51

where the top people were at any given moment. With luck, one or two of the pictures would appear in one of the big national dailies, or an up-market weekly.

Only the palm trees the size of a man in their fancy pots seemed untainted by their surroundings. The gnarled trunks signaled curt rejection of any attempt to be familiar, their tough green leaves protected by a layer of dust an eighth of an inch thick. The tablecloths on the twenty-yard-long tables along both long sides of the hall, originally a dazzling white, were dirty and covered with brown stains. The piles of smoked salmon or eel sandwiches, the egg halves filled with peeled prawns, the ripe gorgonzola and camembert were no more; the dishes of cocktail sausages and meatballs, and even the bowls of mixed salad were empty. All that was left were a few curled triangles of brown bread coated with goose-liver pâté substitute and speared by a toothpick weighed down by a tired grape.

Empty glasses and half-empty plates were dotted around the tables and on every conceivable ledge all over the hall. The palm pots were overflowing with cigarette butts and crumpled napkins, and even the floor was covered with stains and crumbs. A pink-cheeked kitchen boy was busy sweeping up the bits of broken glass and china some over-enthusiastic party guest had managed to knock down.

The waiters, immaculately uniformed and hardened by the experience of hundreds of similar occasions, were stationed strategically about the room like sentries, waiting for the signal from the headwaiter that signified the party was over and the clearing-up process could begin. The only people still working were the bartenders at the three liquid refreshment counters strategically situated in the corners of the hall. The men behind the bar were still polite, but not quite as attentive as they had been.

The festive pomp and carefully measured gallantry, displayed when the doors were first opened some hours previously and the initial pleasantries exchanged, had by now been replaced by a more down-to-earth approach. The two government ministers and all eight ambassadors had left long ago, and their example had soon been followed by other experienced and hardened party-goers. A quarter of an hour earlier the exhibition manager had donned a fixed smile and left the premises, followed by the board and their ladies. The chosen few, destined to be happy for the rest of the evening, would be served dinner in his own dining room. His nod to the headwaiter had given the latter the responsibility of taking over command and sounding the retreat.

A hundred or so guests were left, the private soldiers representing legations and trade delegations, and the occasional man in charge of a stand, looking for an opposite number of either sex from the in-crowd, whose unwritten instructions make it clear he has no business to leave a party until he is thrown out.

Gerd Angerbo loved the annual cocktail party thrown by the exhibition center. For her, there was only one occasion to beat it, and to be honest, that would beat anything. Her secret dream, sweet beyond compare, was to receive an invitation bearing the royal coat-of-arms and postmarked the Royal Palace. Several times every year, the king of Sweden hosts a dinner party for prominent citizens, and as it is difficult to find a sufficient number of outstanding women, Gerd considered her chances of entering the realm of the chosen few rather good. The day would surely come when she could no longer be overlooked.

As Gerd emerged from the ladies rest room, she observed the scene in the hall and found it rather like a street market at the end of a busy day. The boy from the kitchen, having discarded his sweeping brush and replaced it with a floor-cloth, was now crawling among the forest of legs owned by unsteady gentlemen and even less-steady ladies. His face was lobster-red, and when he was finally in a position to get to his feet and gather his paraphernalia together, he could not help but glance at the elegantly dressed gentleman who had been observing his activities all the time, with great interest. The boy was rewarded with a warm and just possibly less-than-innocent smile, accompanied by a jocular wink. The result was even greater embarrassment.

Gerd smiled to herself. The hunting season always gets under way at the end of a party, although she found it difficult to believe that this meticulously correct East German would dare to break with convention and cast off the strait-jacket imposed by strict protocol. Private desires should be satisfied in private, especially if one is number three on the list drawn up by one's own embassy, directly responsible to the ambassador himself and, in this context, the official in charge of the exhibition stand—a female, of course. The Eastern bloc states are very particular about rank, and the lists proffered by the embassy have official status. The same applies in the Swedish monarchy, despite the fact that they do not draw up lists; instead, they take it for granted that everybody knows his place.

The exhibition manager himself had introduced Gerd Angerbo to the East German. As it happened, Herwart Klammer was together with some Russians at the time. One of them was Dr. Dimitri Gusov.

Alf Skolle sauntered across the room, champagne glass in hand, and Gerd noted that he was still relatively steady on his feet. A couple of paces behind him were a couple of guys smiling broadly. There was something ingratiating about them, and she began to catch on to what was coming. Both of them wore mustaches and looked distinctly East European; most striking of all, however, was their obvious exhilaration, suggesting they had been let off the least at last, if only for one evening.

"I was afraid you'd given us the slip," said Skolle, summoning up his most charming smile. "You know I've ordered a table for us in the Old Town. There'll be four of us, actually."

"What a lovely surprise," she responded, without batting an eyelid; she half meant it.

Earlier that evening she had accepted Skolle's invitation to dinner when the party was over—not without misgivings. She was tired of him, his conceit and his dandified behavior. Deep down, she had started to despise him. Not because he stole documents from the ministry and thus supplied her with useful and unique material, establishing himself as a traitor. Not even because he sold himself for money. In this liberated day and age, everyone had the right to do whatever was necessary to make one's life more pleasant. Any suggestion to the contrary was old-fashioned and not worth thinking about. You only live once, and the trick is to sell yourself for the right price. If, against all the odds, you find yourself troubled by a guilty conscience, you can always turn to charity. A conscience is reserved for people who believe, or at least, do not consider that ideologies are dead. Like Gerd Angerbo, Alf Skolle never set foot in church; nor had he been smitten by the infection that sends young people out into the streets to take part in demonstrations.

The reason why Gerd Angerbo had nothing but scorn for Alf Skolle was that she now knew that under the thin man-of-the-world veneer, he was a miserable jerk who had more than once betrayed his panic-stricken terror to her.

The powers-that-be at the exhibition center would, if necessary, accept her excuse for declining Skolle's invitation, despite the fact that it was part of her job to maintain good relations with the ministries and their press secretaries. On the other hand, Dr. Gusov would never accept such childish excuses. He had emphasized more than once the importance of keeping Alf Skolle in a good mood and preventing him from collapsing completely. The Russian often expressed himself in riddles with regard to the way she treated Alf Skolle—it was in fact treatment, rather than a relationship. Gusov had never actually proposed that she should go to bed with Alf Skolle, but after a while it was clear he assumed she had become the press secretary's mistress. This very evening, *en passant,* when they were toasting each other quite formally, he had intimated that her problems would soon be over.

"Let us drink a toast to the spring," he had proposed. "I can assure you it will be early this year."

She had frowned, indicating that she did not really understand his meaning, and so he had moved a little closer.

"Another six weeks, and you can start looking for another lover," he whispered into her ear. "Meanwhile, though, you must make sure your ardor doesn't cool."

There was something regal about Gerd Angerbo when she held out her hand to be kissed by Alf Skolle's hangers-on, one at a time. She had gathered from his introduction that they were both Poles who worked for their country's trade delegation in Stockholm. They declared in unison (and in the remarkable brand of German that Poles are so good at) that they were not only delighted, but also honored beyond all expectation, to be allowed to spend the rest of the evening in the company of such a charming lady.

Without further ado the Poles embarked upon a very earnest but very un-Swedish (albeit polite) conversation with Gerd Angerbo. With Alf Skolle in the lead, and chattering away eagerly, they exited from the party room of the exhibition center, which was now in a state of complete dissolution.

Their departure did not go unnoticed. Herwart Klammer, who seemed to have difficult in dragging himself away (despite the fact that for the past hour he had been unable to find anyone to talk to), observed the departure of the little group with notable discretion. Judging by his satisfied but at the same time ironic expression, it was difficult to work out whether he was fascinated or disturbed by the fact that the two Polish diplomats had decided to keep the evening going at the expense of the two Swedes. Nothing in his expression betrayed whether or not he realized he was not the only one to observe the joint departure of the Swedes and the Poles.

Earlier on, Klammer had noticed two men of early

middle age, obviously Swedish, who seemed to be wandering about at random without actually talking to anyone or meeting a friend. Suddenly the pair of them had become interesting. Okay, Gerd Angerbo was a good-looking woman, and was there a man in this world who would not observe her whenever she showed herself in public? Even so, Klammer was not convinced it was her erotic attraction that had aroused the interest of the two men. When he saw one of them make a slight gesture of the hand in the direction of the door, and the other nod almost imperceptibly, the expression on the East German's face became even more ironic. He turned away without even bothering to confirm that the two Swedes hastened to leave the room within half a minute of each other.

There was nothing surprising or remarkable about the fact that, during the evening, Klammer had been in the same room as two Swedish security officers. Relations between the Republic and the monarchy were such that, despite the favorable circumstances, they had to be regarded as opponents. Even so, Klammer felt he had no reason to be worried; he was convinced they had not been allocated this rather enjoyable mission on his account.

On his way out to the cloakroom Klammer almost bumped into one of the waitresses pushing a serving trolley; by a piece of nimble footwork he managed to avoid a collision. He noticed how she lowered her gaze in embarrassment and politely allowed him to go past. He was almost sure she had actually curtsied. Subservience of that kind never happened back home where, in his opinion, class differences had been eliminated long ago.

Klammer might well have been even more convinced that unlike his own, the capitalist world was short on respect and sympathy for the underprivileged—if only he had turned around. The strikingly short waitress had turned red in the face, and that could have been taken as yet another sign that she belonged to the downtrodden. But it was not out of

57

subservience or embarrassment that her cheeks were glowing so red. In fact, she was furious with herself. For just a couple of seconds, she had entered the visible world. That was inexcusable.

ᏹ6

They had arranged it like a police interrogation, with Gudrun Brunhildson the accused and Frey both interrogator and secretary. He noted all the salient facts (including those that appeared irrelevant) on loose sheets of paper, which he divided into squares, gradually adding headlines. It was essential for everything to be as clear as possible, that nothing was forgotten or overlooked. As yet they did not know the shape and could only guess at the content of the jigsaw puzzle they had started to construct, but it was likely that a few of the pieces would interlock, even at this stage.

Gudrun took it for granted there would be some pieces Frey would keep to himself, without showing her.

When the interrogation was over, they would memorize every little bit of information, no matter how insignificant it might seem. Experience had taught them that the memory functions better if its starting point is notes made in one's own handwriting. Two brains can also remember more than one, and the combined sum of their information is always greater than if each individual memory bank is added together separately. Later that evening, Frey would burn the notes and flush the ashes down the toilet.

"So SÄPO was there," noted Frey, without emotion.

"Four of them," said Gudrun. "Three men and a woman. One of the men and the woman are always there for international trade fairs. They made no attempt to disguise who they were. Several of the guests even went up and said hello. They are there to watch for terrorists and other loonies. The Israeli ambassador also had a bodyguard with him, as usual."

"The other two?"

"From surveillance."

"Do you think Klammer caught on to them?"

"Of course. He even tried to start a conversation with one of them. It didn't get off the ground because of language problems. Klammer spoke German, and you could see how pleased he was when the policeman was forced to shake his head and mutter an apology in bad English. The poor fellow looked really put out."

"Klammer is cheeky, and also rash. He seems to like playing with fire."

"Both cheeky and bold. I rather like him at times. He wanted to find out if he was the one they were after, and he succeeded in doing that. I can guarantee that, for the moment at least, Klammer is of no interest to SÄPO."

"So there was someone else they were keeping an eye on. Any idea who?"

Gudrun hesitated before answering. Then she shook her head doubtfully.

"It could have been either one of two," she said. "Or perhaps both. One of them's a press secretary named Alf Skolle—his minister was there at the party. Skolle's a good-looking fellow who's starting to go to seed, and he drinks too much. He seems to have something going with the other one. Her name's Gerd Angerbo. Information officer at the exhibition center."

60

Frey looked up, and suddenly seemed put out.

"Do you know her?" Gudrun's nostrils were twitching slightly. She sensed she was on to something.

Frey was aware that she was watching him, and that she would not let herself be fobbed off. Instead of answering immediately, he took out a cigarette and made a big fuss of lighting it, as if he were about to give a lengthy explanation. He was quite sure she would not accept just any old yarn.

"I know who she is," he replied, his voice full of seriousness, "and I'm surprised to hear that SÄPO could be at all interested in her, except as a contact. I've spoken to her. I sometimes have to go the exhibition center on some newspaper job or other. She's always been very correct and very helpful, and I know she has quite a good reputation among the journalists. She's a splendid woman, incidentally!"

"She's a bitch!"

Gudrun smiled, and her smile might have been just slightly malicious. He was sure she was not satisfied with his answer. Although he had not actually said anything at all, he knew the clever little woman opposite had seen through him and was beginning to understand. Nevertheless, he had no choice. It was not because he did not trust her. He did not tell her the truth for reasons of security. At the same time, he knew he did not need to say any more, because she would never of her own accord suggest that there was any connection between him and Gerd Angerbo. She knew the rules and was prepared to observe them at all times.

There was nothing to add. Frey put down his cigarette and picked up his pen again.

"Apart from that, I've had nothing to do with her," he lied tamely. "I don't know Skolle at all."

The latter claim was true.

"In any case, it was either Angerbo or Skolle that SÄPO was interested in," said Gudrun. "Incidentally, they're in the Old Town just now, having dinner with a couple of Poles."

"That might explain why . . ." suggested Frey in all too

61

enthusiastic attempt to divert her suspicions. She interrupted him immediately.

"No. The Poles have nothing to do with it."

She made it quite clear she was in no mood to let him go wandering off unnecessarily down blind alleys. Her expression had clouded over, and he was keen to avoid sparking off a thunderstorm.

"We both need a whiskey," said Frey, getting to his feet.

It was an attempt to defuse the situation. To his relief, she nodded in agreement; she was still aggressive, but no longer as hostile. They both accepted they needed a few minutes of silence in order to think things over.

While he was puttering about in the kitchen, playing for time, he hoped she would have got over her disappointment. She knew he had lied to her. He sometimes forgot she was a woman, and not neuter like him, at least as far as emotions were concerned. Nothing would have been gained by his starting to tell her the full story. Actually, there was not much he could allow himself to tell her. For her sake, it was safest for him to keep quiet about Gerd Angerbo. Gudrun would want him to say nothing about her if the roles were reversed. Silence and keeping quiet were the wall that separated them, but it also united them. Neither of them could afford to try and scale that barrier without risking the other's continued existence.

All the same, he was annoyed with himself. He ought to have realized her hypersensitive instincts and astonishing powers of intuition would put her on the right track. It was a poor excuse to claim he had been taken by surprise, almost stumped. Just for a moment, he had let the mask fall and revealed his naked and no doubt terrified face. It was the threat that had caused the mask to slip. If SÄPO was interested in Gerd Angerbo, that must mean it had got uncomfortably close to him as well. Much too close. It was a small and, in this connection, irrelevant consolation to know that SÄPO could not care less what Herwart Klammer from the German Democratic Republic was up to in Stockholm, not yet at least. The alarm bells were ringing, and very loudly at that, and neither he nor Gudrun Brunhildson had any chance of getting out of earshot, or even looking for a better hiding place.

She smiled at him when he returned, and sat quite still when he stroked her hair tenderly and kissed the lobe of her ear. They sat drinking for a while, as if the silence and the keeping quiet was binding them together once more. There was no longer any noticeable discord between them—they would never allow it to occur.

"It was an evening full of surprises," said Gudrun eventually, with great seriousness. "I got the impression Klammer was also interested in Skolle and Angerbo. He wasn't exactly keeping watch on them, but he was never far away from them either. It seemed as if he was making sure they left before he did."

"Are you sure?"

"It's also possible, of course, that Klammer was just hanging around to make certain SÄPO was not in fact after him."

Frey shook his head in annoyance. He looked really irritated.

"Once again, I can't understand what's going on," he said sullenly. "Is there a link between Klammer, Skolle, and Angerbo?"

"It depends what you mean. I'm quite sure neither Skolle nor the lady in question has any mutual business with Klammer, not even any interest in his existence. I'm not sure whether the reverse is true, though."

"What do you mean?"

"Klammer stayed at the exhibition center for nearly two hours. He was one of the first to arrive, and one of the last to leave. He spent the first half hour making polite conversation, and then he was on his own. Anybody who was somebody left the party after an hour, at most. Even the exhibition manager had had enough. And yet, Klammer stayed on—and not just because of the drink."

"You said he might have been wanting to wait until SÄPO had left."

"That's a pretty farfetched idea, in fact. Klammer is an expert at getting rid of shadows. If I didn't know he was staying with you, I'd have lost him every day. Incidentally, he never bothers to try and hide where he's going at first."

"At first?"

"Exactly. Klammer's journey home is divided into two stages. The first stage is as open as you like, and the address is always the same."

"And that is?" he asked patiently.

"The East German embassy, of course. That's where he changes trains, as it were. It's only later, several hours later when he starts heading for your place, that he begins getting awkward."

"Maybe he had other plans for tonight."

Once again, there was a glint in Gudrun's eye, and he had the impression she felt insulted. She was very sensitive to criticism when her anticipation and job loyalty were concerned. To his relief, she took her thick, blond hair in both hands and lifted it up to reveal her slender neck as she burst into laughter.

"No," she said contemptuously. "He certainly did not."

"You mean . . ." His astonishment was genuine. "How can you be so sure?"

"Trade secret!" she teased him. "I stood waiting in the cold for at least half an hour before he turned up at the embassy. For some reason, Herwart Klammer seems to like Stockholm's public transport. I'd go as far as to say that he's an expert on it already, and that's the only reason he came to Sweden. I haven't been able to find any other, at least. Buses, trains, the underground—he's tried the lot. How he gets there, in any case, is on the complicated side. My mode of transport was arranged in advance, though."

"You're matchless."

"Dutiful," she replied with a smile. "It would have looked very nice, wouldn't it, if I'd slipped up tonight and missed our first check-up session. I expect I'd have been told off."

"By me?" Frey shook his head disarmingly.

"No," he assured her gently, "I couldn't afford to do that. I don't know anybody who compares with you."

"Rubbish," she replied, but he saw she was blushing, and it was obvious she was pleased with the praise.

"How come you managed to get away from your waitress job so quickly?"

"Oh, that was fixed as well. The restaurants at the exhibition center always have trouble getting staff because they're only open now and then. It's especially hard when it comes to parties in the evening, and they don't employ any old riffraff. I'd only promised to be there for the first hour. The headwaiter was very pleased to see that I stayed longer than I said I would, and he asked me to come back tomorrow, Saturday. That's the last day of the trade fair. Not just for me, but for Klammer as well."

"Has Klammer been to the fair every day since he came to Stockholm?"

"He spends the night at your place, and his days at the fair. He doesn't get involved in the work at the East German stand. It often looks as though he has trouble passing the time. In fact, he keeps out of the way, and most of the day he just sits in their private office and stares into space."

"How strange."

"Most of all, he tries to avoid meeting businessmen. He doesn't always succeed."

Frey noticed immediately that her voice had become more tense, and he realized she was about to reveal the last and most interesting piece of the jigsaw.

"That sounds odd."

"But understandable, perhaps," said Gudrun.

"What do you mean?"

"Yesterday I happened to overhear a conversation between two Swedish businessmen who had been doing some deal or other with the East Germans. I hung around for a while without them noticing me. That's quite easy to do at the fair; the aisles between the stands are like back alleys, and it's hellishly crowded everywhere. One of the Swedes was quite put out, if not downright upset. He'd evidently come to the fair in order to meet with Herwart Klammer, and been directed to our friend."

"And . . ."

Her eyes sparkled, and he could see she was enjoying leading him on, even though it was only for a few seconds. He let her have that pleasure. It was her way of establishing that all those long hours of waiting and days of strict concentration and constant awareness, watching out for the unexpected, had not been in vain.

"It was the wrong man," she replied, purely and simply. "Our Herwart Klammer is not the Herwart Klammer the Swede had met in Leipzig six months ago."

"He might have mixed the names up—there are thousands of Klammers in Germany and Austria."

"That's exactly what the Swede's friend said, but he was quite definite and insisted there was no possibility of a mistake. He'd met Klammer in a bar in Leipzig, and they'd started talking and got on pretty well. The East German said he would be going to Stockholm in connection with the trade fair. The next day they'd gone on a trip to Dresden and had lunch together, and when they separated, they even exchanged addresses. The Swede had promised to look after the East German when he came to Sweden."

This time Frey's silence was understandable.

"Got any suspicions?" he asked, eventually.

"The same as you," she replied. "But where's the proof?"

Frey shook his head. He look thoughtful, and more composed than before.

"I'm astonished," he said, but there was no hint of desperation in his voice and his surprise was controlled. "You'd never think this sort of thing would ever happen in real life," he went on. "The risks seem to be too great."

"I agree entirely," she said. "You always have to reckon with coincidence, and that's impossible to forecast."

"It wasn't just coincidence which led you to overhear that conversation. Anyway, there are now three people at least who know that there are two Herwart Klammers in Stockholm."

"No. Just two. You and me. The Swede was going to write to Leipzig and ask for an explanation. He's one of those types who have too many fingers in too many pies. Anyway, no one would take him seriously if he turned to the authorities. Thousands of addresses are written down in bars all over the world every night, and more than half of them are false."

"So the real Herwart Klammer is sitting in the embassy playing patience all day long," said Frey. "SÄPO checked him in when he arrived at Arlanda Airport, and they'll check him out when he goes home again. Other SÄPO men have been checking him out at the fair, just as they've done with hundreds of foreigners. Nobody has noticed the switch, and it's not difficult to see why, in fact. They probably just have lists that they tick off."

"It's the same for them as for us: They need advance information if they are to act. That's not the case with Klammer."

"Are you sure we're not making a mistake?" he asked.

"You can never rule out a mistake," replied Gudrun, and she felt as if he were listening to himself speak. As if he had been correcting himself.

"Mistakes can be made good," he countered.

"Of course," she said, and smiled again. "They're going home on Monday. The East German plane leaves around two o'clock. I'll be at the airport in good time."

"Good. That's two days away. We'll just have to wait in the meantime."

They sat there quietly for a few minutes, thinking things over. Even if they still did not understand much of what was happening—and the presence of two Herwart Klammers in Stockholm complicated the overall pattern somewhat—they still felt they had moved forward a little bit.

"You'd better be very careful in the future," said Frey earnestly. "You mustn't take any risks. I won't pretend I understand what's going on, but I have my suspicions, and I fear we're both in danger."

"Nobody will ever know I've been following Herwart Klammer's namesake to the plane to make sure he got away safely."

"What do you have in mind?"

"The first thing is to find out whether there is a Herwart Klammer booked on the flight to East Berlin next Monday."

"How will you do that?"

"All foreigners go shopping in Sweden, or at least all those from the Eastern bloc do. As you know, whatever they buy is free of Swedish taxes. Some firms even have personnel at the airport to ensure their customers receive their tax refund."

Frey bust out laughing.

"I get it," he said.

He stood up, walked around the table, and kissed her on the mouth. It was not just that he wanted to put a stop to the conversation and avoid having to speculate out loud about what the East German was doing in Stockholm, but he really was taken by her. Perhaps he was even in love with her.

"What would I do without you?" he asked.

"You'd find somebody else," she replied, impishly. "I've no doubt you've got at least one more in reserve."

"You overestimate me." He smiled.

He took a pace back from the table, and she could see

straightaway from his eyes, his mouth, and his smile what he was going to say next.

"Have you any objection to my letting our anonymous East German friend spend the night all alone in my apartment?"

She tried to look doubtful, but was not particularly successful.

"I thought you preferred other bedmates," she complained, provocatively.

"You don't really think that at all," said Jonas Mikael Frey.

A few hours later, when they had smoked their last cigarette and put out the bedside lamp, Gudrun raised herself up on one elbow and thumped Frey in the chest.

"There's something I forgot to tell you," she said.

"What's that?" he inquired drowsily.

"Herwart Klammer likes small boys with down on their cheeks," she sniggered girlishly. "Especially if their voices have just broken."

"Rather him than me," said Frey with a grunt. "Has he had any luck?"

"Not yet. He hasn't even tried properly. But he will. I've seen it in his eyes."

"As long as he doesn't bring them back to my apartment, I'm not going to interfere in his sex life, no matter how disgusting it might be."

"He won't do that," said Gudrun, sinking down into her pillow. "But at least it shows he has a weakness. And," she went on thoughtfully, "weaknesses are there to be exploited."

⁊7

On this, the first Monday in February, a deep depression moved into Scandinavia from the west, quite unexpectedly, and reached as far as the Stockholm area. Wet snow started falling in large lumps that immediately froze and formed icy patches on high ground. The result was traffic chaos, and in the capital itself snow clearance teams were fighting what appeared to be a vain battle with the slush that threatened to overwhelm the streets and squares of Stockholm. At Arlanda Airport all flights were canceled. Visibility was nil, and no sooner had the enormous snowblowers laboriously cleared the landing strips than they were snowed under again.

For many people the change in the weather was a relief, in spite of everything. The youngest citizens suddenly had an opportunity to exercise their creative talents, and in every school playground hard-working and independent groups of artists built one snowman after another. They were all more or less identical, and faithful copies of the first prototype made many centuries previously. Nevertheless, there was one noticeable innovation that some people found provocative: The enlightened youth of today had liberated their snowmen from their traditional sexlessness, and endowed their creations with unmistakable and prominent indications of their manhood. There was not a snowwoman to be seen, which was probably a reflection of the disappearance of the old wooden broom from modern domestic life.

Out in the streets, people were slithering about with a smile on their lips and their collars wide open in an attempt to rid themselves of the excess heat generated under their thick woolen underwear, well-padded fur coats, and thick Greenland sweaters. It was obvious they had started to hope that even this confounded winter was not going to drape them in gloom for ever and ever. Somewhere not far ahead, the rejuvenating and hormone-inducing spring was lying in wait, and in a couple of months, three at the most, life could start all over again. Instead of this bitter winter, people would be able to enjoy spring colds and hay fever. But the dream of approaching summer would prove to be more than a vain illusion.

There were people who were making a fortune out of the weather. The men operating the snowplows, the roof-clearers and their assistants shouting out orders in the street below, were all earning big money. To some extent, these workers were recruited from the ranks of those who normally fight shy of any kind of paid work. They were not exactly signing on for these jobs out of altruistic social consciousness; their motives were more crass. They knew they would not need to exert themselves unduly, and that no one would complain about their substantial claims for overtime. The highways commission was under heavy pressure and, ignoring the disapproving objections that would no doubt arrive in time from the tax authorities, it accepted the offers of help they were receiving from farmers driving their own tractors and from newly formed but, as so often in the past, surprisingly short-lived firms of haulage contractors specializing in snow removal.

71

Restaurants and bars that had been deserted for weeks started to fill up with cheerful, red-cheeked people, and the cloakroom attendants started to rub their hands together once again. Their cramped cubbyholes were bulging at the seams thanks to the mass of heavy, wet winter clothes and copious fur coats.

It was as if the city had managed to wriggle its way out of its straitjacket.

For a lot of people, however, the change in the weather caused nothing but problems and inconvenience. And for others, it was a disappointment. Gudrun could very well understand that Herwart Klammer, the real Herwart Klammer she was out to expose, thought he had good grounds for feeling miserable. His shopping tour of central Stockholm had come to nothing. For the previous week or more he had sat there, locked in the East German embassy, and not even been allowed to wander around this capitalist city with its excess of luxury goods and shamelessly seductive products. This was his first excursion west and north of the river Elbe and, as it turned out, his only visit to the other side of the barbed wire and minefields protecting his homeland from the decadent influence and threat of attack from the West.

Loyal comrades of Herwart Klammer's sort are always worthy of both encouragement and gratitude. There are more strenuous missions than sitting in an embassy guest room for ten days, it is true, but all the same, even sitting still, if it incorporates meaningful passivity, deserves a reward. From the moment he had arrived in Stockholm, Herwart Klammer had been promised three epicurean hours of absolute freedom in NK, PUB, or any other big store in this haven of capitalistic frivolity. All in return for not asking any questions, and not saying a word about what really happened when he went to Stockholm.

Late on Sunday evening the ambassador himself had entertained Klammer in lighthearted conversation and handed over a substantial sum in Swedish currency, to be spent exactly as he wished. It was intended as a balm to soothe the aches and pains acquired as a result of sitting on the ambassador's artificial leather sofa. When he got back to East Berlin, Klammer would be able to show off to his friends and family a Swedish-made video recorder, one of the most cherished status symbols in the whole of the Socialist world. After that, no one would ever question whatever he had to tell them about life and living standards in the kingdom of Sweden.

And now the snow had ruined everything. As early as half past eight on Monday morning, Klammer was forced to break off his preparations for his shopping spree, and instead found himself in a car with three of his fellow-countrymen, sliding and slithering through the slush and ice to Arlanda. Under no circumstances must they miss the plane to Schönefeld.

It took them over two hours to reach the airport, and having got there, they were greeted with the depressing news that all flights were canceled for the foreseeable future. Klammer was exasperated to find that the only change as far as he was concerned was that he had left one prison for another. His spirits were well below zero, and he was determined he would never again allow himself to be talked into accepting a foreign trip on similar terms. Stockholm, Spitsbergen, London—they could take a running jump.

Gudrun knew all about Klammer's misfortune. She had followed the East German car out to Arlanda, and made sure at the same time that there was no one else on the same mission. The driving skills of the uniformed chauffeur on the snow-covered roads were not exactly outstanding, and Gudrun was not exactly surprised when she saw the CD-plated car end up in a ditch shortly after the Märsta exit—there had been any number of close calls during the twenty-mile drive. The landing was comparatively soft, and no one was in danger of being hurt, so Gudrun drove on and completed the remaining three miles to the airport without a second thought. She had to wait over an hour before the shivering and decidedly irritated comrades showed up at the entrance, accompanied by a grim-faced man in the most garish orange overalls imaginable. He was the driver of the rescue vehicle that had pulled them out of the ditch, and it was quite clear he had no intention of leaving the group of East Germans until they had paid him for his services.

Gudrun had no difficulty at all in working out which of the four was Herwart Klammer. She eliminated the driver without more ado: He was instructed to take a seat in the café and wait until the plane for Berlin had taken off. He left without any sign of protest, and seemed to have nothing against being left to his own devices. The woman with the ossified expression and the sewn-up lips had been in charge of the stand at the fair. She left no one in doubt about her contempt for the way in which capitalists looked after their roads, and looked as if she could not wait to get home again. That left the two men, one of whom was very correct-looking and gray-haired, in his sixties, who seemed very much at home among the escalators and corridors. He assumed command immediately, and led the way to the restaurant. The third man slouched along behind, his head bowed, looking as if he had been expelled to Siberia. That just had to be Herwart Klammer.

A little over an hour later Gudrun was presented with the opportunity she had been waiting for. The East Germans had finished their lunch and ordered coffee, and the elder of the two men rose to his feet and made it clear he was going to inquire about the weather, and find out if there was any point in their waiting. He was accompanied by the sneering woman, who headed for the ladies' rest room. The third man was left all alone at the table.

The man Gudrun assumed must be Herwart Klammer had turned his back on the other diners and was staring fixedly if indignantly out of the big picture window. The blizzard had eased, and it looked as if it might soon stop snowing. So much for his hopes! He had been hoping for some time now that the loudspeakers would announce the cancellation of all flights from Arlanda until tomorrow. If only they would make such a decision, he would still be able to buy his precious video recorder. The brick-colored thousand-kronor notes were still in his wallet; the ambassador had omitted to ask for them back in the rush to leave the embassy. They would be of no use at all to him in Berlin, as he would be forced to hand them back to the Foreign Office.

"Herr Klammer?"

The man by the window came to with a start and looked in surprise at the little woman who had suddenly appeared by his table, smiling shyly.

"Yes," he muttered, morosely.

"Herr Herwart Klammer?"

"That's right."

He stared at her in surprise and grasped the edge of the table involuntarily with one hand. Surely no one apart from customs officials and the embassy staff could possibly know he was in Stockholm.

"I'm very sorry to disturb you," said Gudrun in a friendly tone, her German sounding much worse than she was capable of if she really tried.

"The people at the fair have sent me to give you this little souvenir of Stockholm and to thank you for your interest in this year's exhibition. You ought really to have had it at the reception on Friday, but I'm afraid it got overlooked."

Klammer was surprised, one might almost say dismayed, to find himself presented with a little square box, neatly wrapped in shiny gold paper with a bright blue ribbon and a fancy rosette. The exhibition manager's visiting card was tucked into the rosette and held in place by a pin with a head depicting St. Erik, said to be the founder of Stockholm and now regarded as the patron saint of the city.

"What's all this then?" asked Klammer in bewilderment.

"I'm sorry, I've no idea," answered Gudrun. "I'm just the messenger girl."

She smiled her innocent smile, as if she was apologizing for her very existence. She curtsied slightly but noticeably as she took her leave. Klammer stared thoughtfully after her as she walked to the door, but after a few seconds, his face cleared and he breathed a sigh of relief.

The brief but heartfelt message from the exhibition manager was surely no more than a routine gesture. He had no doubt given away dozens of similar souvenirs over the last few days. That kind of publicity stunt was normal at nearly all trade fairs, and for some reason or other, Klammer's gift had been overlooked. As a special gesture, someone had arranged for a messenger girl to take it to the airport for him—that was just the kind of VIP treatment that visitors generally appreciated. They might even have planned it that way from the start. There was no need to start worrying about the girl; as far as she was concerned, he was just a foreign name and a vague face, one of many during a busy week. She had not doubted for a moment that he was the person he claimed to be. Most probably the headwaiter would have helped her to find him. Klammer was quite sure there were no other Germans in the restaurant just then.

Only a careless man takes unnecessary risks, and during his visit to Stockholm, Klammer had become much more careful than he had been before. No one had given him a satisfactory explanation as to why he had been kept under house arrest at the embassy, but nevertheless, they had sworn him to silence at the same time as hinting his future career would benefit as a result of his loyal cooperation. There was no need to lecture him on the consequences of speaking out of turn, or of stepping out of line. And so Klammer put the little box away in his briefcase with a nod—he would open it when he got home. No need to mention to his traveling companions that the fair people had sent him a souvenir. They would be able to say quite honestly that he had played his part in Stockholm perfectly.

Only two hours later the flight for Schönefeld took off from Arlanda. The blizzard had moved on, and in its wake were glittering crystals of melting snow and the danger of roof falls. One lone figure watched the passengers embark on the flight to East Germany. The sun was peering out from behind the clouds, and from her vantage point in the observation lounge, Gudrun Brunhildson had no trouble observing the passengers as they boarded. She noted with a satisfied smile that Herwart Klammer was one of the first up the steps. Before taking the escalator down to the main hall, she watched the uneventful takeoff through her binoculars. Shortly afterward, as she got into her car and prepared to drive back into Stockholm, she was able to state categorically that Herwart Klammer was no longer on Swedish soil. Only his namesake was still in Sweden, and possibly also his identity papers.

⌇8   Although it was already well past eleven in the morning, both Gerd Angerbo and Alf Skolle were still in bed. Each in his or her own bed, a respectable distance apart in their respective parts of the city. Neither of them was troubled by the bad weather.

A few hours previously, his reluctant, trembling fingers had managed to dial the number of the ministry, and he had informed them he had been smitten by the severe influenza that had been creating havoc in Stockholm for some time. The personnel manager himself took the call, and was instantly convinced of the seriousness of the illness that, he felt, needed a week in bed. He had only to hear Skolle's hoarse, grating voice to conclude that its owner was right about the diagnosis and suggested treatment. The personnel manager could only hope Skolle would soon be better, and he was sincere when he added some well-meaning advise as to the best treatment. Nothing is any good for influenza except household remedies. Though they would not admit it to their patients, even doctors drink red wine punch when they have flu, or stand with a towel over their heads, breathing in the

78

fumes of various concoctions. The personnel manager had always had a soft spot for the press secretary, whose easygoing nature was a pleasant change from the self-centered careerist attitude of the minister himself. It never occurred to him that Skolle's claims of illness were a pack of lies. They were, however.

Skolle was in a poor way, certainly, but he did not have a temperature and his hoarseness was due to an excess of cigarettes during the last few days. In addition, he had a hangover, and consequently had a headache that had thus far resisted all attempts to counter it with a constant flow of aspirins.

The real reason Skolle had not the strength to go to the office lay deeper than that. After the dinner with Gerd Angerbo and the Poles, he had expected a pleasant sequel at Gerd's apartment, but for the first time ever, she had resisted his advances. They had quarreled for a while, but there was no changing her mind, and in the end, she had sent him packing in a way that made it clear she had nothing but contempt for him. He had taken a taxi home, gone to bed, and awoken the next morning in a furious temper that he had immediately proceeded to drown in a licensed snack bar. He had continued all weekend, apart from the hours he had spent in his own bed, stupefied and out to the world. By midnight on Sunday he was so drunk again that not a single bar in the whole of Stockholm would let him in. Back home he found a drop of gin and downed it with an ecstatic sigh of relief as if to suggest it had saved his life.

It can sometimes happen that a very drunk person is suddenly blessed with insight. Standing by the kitchen sink with a tumbler full to overflowing with lukewarm, acrid gin, Skolle started talking to himself. He was both plaintiff and defendant. The conversation was frank, and both parties attempted to establish the honest truth. It was as if he were listening in from the outside, the only occupant of the public gallery. The prosecution refrained from making reproaches, and the defendant tried to avoid the tearful self-pity that had completely dominated Skolle's behavior only a few hours previously.

The first question concerned what he was actually engaged in.

"Spying," answered Skolle, without a trace of hesitation and, indeed, with an undertone of pride.

"Pretty skillful spying at that, dammit," he added after a few moments gazing into space, wide-eyed. "An excellent job. Badly paid, though."

He grinned. He'd soon put that right.

"You've started drinking."

That was a surprisingly brutal assertion, which resulted in a grim face and pursed lips. But it was true.

"If you don't stop, you'll be found out."

What ridiculous logic! It could result in his getting the sack, that was true enough. But getting found out, no! There was no connection between his drinking and the risk of being discovered. He was always sober when at work. Nearly always.

"Only second-rate spies get caught," rejoined Skolle, defiantly. "Who could possibly catch me?"

"You could be betrayed."

"By Gerd?!"

That was a stupid suggestion if ever he'd heard one. He could not help laughing at himself.

"She's just as dependent on my silence as I am on hers. Perhaps more so."

"There are others who could give you away."

"Who? Only Gerd knows what I do."

"You've only her word for that. You're surely not naive enough to believe everything she tells you?"

He searched for a convincing-sounding reply. It did not need to be crushing, but he wished he could find one that was at least reassuring.

"Ridiculous," he muttered, semiaudibly. "Even if she has

passed on my name and they've heard of me in Moscow or Warsaw or where the hell, there's no proof. We haven't got a contract. Nothing in writing, no receipts. I haven't been as naive as that."

Skolle thumped the table with his fist, and somehow managed to prevent the glass of gin from overturning. No, he had never been naive. Nor stupid, come to that.

"I suppose she might lie to me now and then," he continued aloud, trying to convince himself. "Maybe she does play-act all the time. Like some kind of Mata Hari. So what? That proves nothing. Not that she's going to betray me, in any case. To whom, anyway? And above all, why? Gerd Angerbo will never find an agent as good as I am. Somebody who walks the corridors of power like I do. No, the reverse is true! She has to look after me. In every way she can. She has to cosset me with the same kind of loving care and attention you tend a rare orchid in the middle of winter."

Skolle's face exuded satisfaction. His eyes were gleaming, and he was pleased with his metaphor. Besides, it sounded logical and authentic. Not quite foolproof, though.

"You quarreled last Friday."

"That was nothing."

It was irrelevant. Women use that kind of tactic occasionally.

"We'll forget all about it," said Skolle aloud.

"You find it easy to forget things," countered the other voice, ironically. "You look the other way when something unpleasant happens. What do you really know about this kind of thing?"

"I know that no intelligence service in the world can afford to let its top agents down. Everybody knows that. The whole organization would burst like a punctured balloon."

"That's just something you've read about. Spy thrillers are made up. Reality is something else. Ruthless and scheming. Inhuman, on the whole."

"How can you know that?"

A brilliant answer. Take anybody down a peg or two. Intelligent, superior. What else is there to say? Even when you are talking to yourself, you have to recognize there comes a point when there's nothing more to be said.

Silence. Complete, almost scary silence. Only when he had stoked up confidence by half-emptying his glass of gin and, not without difficulty, lit another cigarette was Skolle ready to make new assertions.

"You're scared," he said, condescendingly. "You can't deny you're damned scared. That's why you're drinking. If no one is going to betray you, why are you afraid? Are you going to let them catch you in the act, and who is after you anyway?"

It was a good question. No one was after him. Not as far as he knew, suspected, or could feel. Still, the question had to be answered. That was the question to conclude the whole conversation. The core of it all. The reason why he had got into his present state.

"I don't know," he mumbled, and his voice had lost all its strength. "Sometimes I just get that nasty feeling. I can't explain it. Maybe . . ."

"Maybe what?"

The gin glass was empty, and with it, Skolle's head was empty as well. He bent over the filthy kitchen table with his head in his hands, rubbing his fevered brow with his fingertips. After a while, he started crying. Quietly at first, and sobbing like a lost child, then more and more violently, as if he had been stricken by great sorrow. In between, he kept mumbling incomprehensively to himself, but there was no one listening anymore.

"Much too simple," he whispered, sniffing loudly. "Incredible . . . simple . . . almost lax . . ."

"Trust," he sighed after a while, as if the answer was torturing him. "Greater and greater trust . . . that's what they're offering . . . damn me if that's not what they're offering . . ."

Then before the explosion came in his head and he lost consciousness, his gaze wandering all over the white kitchen wall in front of him as if he were expecting a reply rather than just an echo, desperate, but spirited even so:

"Not just the minister . . . but . . . him as well . . . the section head. . . ."

When he woke up the next morning, his bedfellows were Angst and Regret. After ringing the personnel manager at the office, he hid his head under the blankets once more. He could remember very little of the last couple of days on the booze, and recalled only vague but painful fragments of his nocturnal monologue. He did not want to be reminded about it all, and so he shut his eyes and sank back into a dreamless doze, as if searching for mercy. But there was no absolution to be found. Only when the telephone woke him and he realized it was afternoon was Skolle forced to give way to reality.

Gerd Angerbo was greeted with cheerful shouts when she turned up at the exhibition center shortly after lunch. Her cheeks were glowing with health and the effect of the winter cold, and she was wearing a newly purchased fur jacket that was examined and admired by the girls in the office. Apart from the staff supervising the clearing of the exhibition halls and the two telephone operators on duty in reception, nearly everybody was in the coffee room. Someone had provided a cake, and there were two bottles of port on the table. The bosses were conspicuous by their absence—everyone knew they were having drinks in the manager's office. The red light on the door had been on for several hours now. The industrial fair had been an undeniable success, and there was every excuse to make the most of the occasion and enjoy the achievement.

On a day like this—the first quiet day after a week of hard work, stress, and limited but not always paid over-time—it would never have occurred to the management to intervene and impose discipline. One or two exhibitors, unused to the routine, who had problems in dismantling and removing their equipment were pleasantly surprised by the warmth with which their appeals for help were met at the office, and they had no trouble in obtaining well-qualified assistance. It is natural for a long-distance runner to collapse in a heap and get his breath back after stubbornly completing an exhausting run, and it was just as natural for the exhibition center staff to do the same after their exertions.

Gerd left after half an hour, saying she was going to make a tour of the halls before going back home. That was part of her routine, and a signal to the others that it was time to draw the party to a close. Anyone who could transferred the fun to more private surroundings behind closed doors, preferably ones with a red lamp outside and a drinks cabinet inside for entertainment purposes.

The diesel fumes from the noisy but fast and efficient trucks hung over the vast exhibition halls like a steel-blue cloud. Although the giant doors, the same size and shape as a badminton court, were wide open and the wintry cold was seeping in, the cloud was low: it got up people's noses and into their throats, and most of the workers had tears in their eyes. If Gerd had not had a prearranged appointment, she would have turned around and gone back to the office even before she had reached the bottom of the staircase.

As usual, her presence created a stir. Workmen in dirty overalls downed their files and chisels and paused for a few moments, truck drivers and crane operators relaxed their concentration and waved merrily, and Gerd smiled at them all. She was well aware that the basis of all popularity and good reputations is to be found among those at the bottom of the hierarchy. The managing director has yet to be born who does not take note of a spontaneously expressed compliment about a colleague if it comes from a trade union member. Gerd Angerbo was popular among the ordinary workers, who never even began to suspect that, in fact, she despised them. Being one of the lads when you know you are not is always a put-on show, and is easy to see through if one has an ear for dissonances and is not impressed by excessive simplicity. Moreover, it is an advantage to be an outsider, and most citizens of contemporary Sweden have neither the opportunity, time, or energy to be one.

The Soviet stand was like a protected and virginal haven in the middle of the largest hall. All around the imposing construction, adorned with thought-provoking slogans, it seemed that chaos reigned, although the confusion may well have been a sign of efficiency and good organization. Away from this socialistic free zone, men were on piece work, and everyone seemed to be aware of the fact that time was money.

The Russians had not even started dismantling and removing, but even so, the stand was buzzing with activity and the roped-off area was full of life and movement. Little groups of men and women were busy, or so it seemed, ticking off every item that was to be transported back to the Soviet Union. There was not a single exhibit, advertising board, or piece of furniture, not even a tool, tablecloth, or vase that was not listed, or should have been listed, in the inventory. In charge of operations was a sharp-nosed but plump woman for whom everyone seemed to hold the greatest respect. Everyone involved had pencils and a bundle of duplicated lists in their hands, while the lower-ranking and more proletarian portion of the work force watched what their comradely superiors were doing with amused interest and occasional mocking comments.

Occasionally a bitter quarrel would break out when some object or other proved to be missing—someone would have to admit responsibility for the loss when they got back home. The Swedish removal man had been waiting patiently for hours with his trucks, crane lorries, and packing cases. He was an experienced man and knew how Russian organization worked, and so he was waiting patiently for the inevitable moment when all the controllers would spread out their arms and reluctantly abandon the laborious and frustrating work. There would be far too many items on the list unaccounted for, and the mighty state of peasants and workers would be forced to acknowledge unforeseen financial losses. In fact, most of the deficiency was on paper, since the inventories had never been complete or even correct, but reflected more the ambitions of the organizing committee that had been set up for the purpose, which had naturally refused to give way to the facts of the socialistic way of life.

In the middle of the Russian territory was the office, which was difficult of access for anyone who had not managed to obtain a pass. That was Gerd Angerbo's destination. She smiled sympathetically at a group of Swedish suppliers who had been directed by the guards to some rickety chairs outside the holy of holies. They were queuing up for an opportunity to be paid. Only the sharp-nosed woman's signature would do as authorization, and it was absolutely essential if they were to extract payment from the embassy. Perhaps she was reluctant to hand out any more hard currency since the inadequate budget for the fair fixed in advance in Moscow was long since exceeded. Once she had left Sweden, the chances of their getting paid were more or less nonexistent. That was why all the Swedish businessmen were stubbornly sitting on their chairs, and had been forced to forgo the lunch they badly needed.

Dr. Dimitri Gusov rose to his feet to welcome Gerd Angerbo when she was shown into his office. He seemed cooler and more distant then she had ever seen him before, and she immediately got the feeling something had gone wrong. The Russian indicated a chair in front of his desk with a stiff, military gesture. They were alone in the room, and when the Russian did not open his mouth, Gerd's smile became increasingly stiff and uncertain.

"I am not pleased," said Gusov without warning, and continued to look depressed.

Gerd looked genuinely surprised.

"With me?" she inquired, put out.

"You have been careless." The Russian sounded grim. "You have disobeyed my instructions. I can't allow that kind of behavior."

Gerd shook her head in incomprehension. She had always followed his instructions, or tried to at least. He was often vague and liked to insinuate things.

"There must be some mistake," said Gerd, gulping, and making a brave effort to brighten up her smile.

"Not at all. On Friday night you quarreled in public with Alf Skolle. Outside a very well-known restaurant. Too many people saw you. You were not exactly low-voiced and expressed yourself in a way that could be described as regrettable, to say the least. In the end, you took a taxi and left him alone in the street. The next day, you gave him a telling off on the telephone, and the consequence was he started drinking."

"How can you possibly know . . . ?"

She broke off in the middle of the sentence and frowned, only to become aware immediately afterward of the evil glint in the Russian's eye.

"I know everything," claimed Dr. Gusov in a voice that boded no contradiction. "It's my job to know. Your only task is to obey orders."

"But just a minute . . ." She sighed. "I do nothing else," she said softly. "Can't you understand that? The fact is I'm fed up with Skolle. He's a pain in the neck. I sometimes feel as if I were his sugar daddy."

"That's exactly what you are."

She looked surprised.

"We have agreed that . . ." she started in a conscious attempt to assert herself.

"That you should be his bit of fluff," interrupted the Russian crudely. "Bit of fluff and sugar daddy. Both at the same time. You can't complain about the pay."

Gerd blushed. She was ruffled, and felt as if he had

87

struck her. Bit of fluff. She hated the expression. She could never imagine that . . .

"Alf Skolle has taken a whole week's leave," announced Gusov in a more objective tone of voice. "He blames it on influenza. The timing is most inconvenient. Your job is to make sure he is back at work within the next three days."

"If he's ill, they'll send him back home again."

"His sickness is in the soul, not in his tubes," said Gusov, looking very Russian. "He feels let down. By you. He's lonely and miserable. That's why you must get him to think differently. You have access to the right means—use them! What Alf Skolle needs is a little orgy. Give him one, and don't hang back. But go easy on the hard liquor."

It sounded like a threat. For the first time since she got to know Gusov, she felt frightened. Their relationship had thus far been free of this kind of insinuation. The Russian had always been very polite and not pushy in any way. Despite the fact that their topics of conversation had frequently been intricate, he often seemed harmless and naive. As time went by, their relations had become more correct and businesslike, but he had never been headstrong. Gerd had gradually got the impression she was superior to her contact man in most respects. Dr. Gusov could sometimes give an almost ridiculous, not to say infantile, impression, but she felt he was more like an accountant than anything else. The kind of accountant who appears in books, at least. A little man who obeys orders and endeavors anxiously not to lose his job. That is why Gerd had begun to suspect that Gusov was no more than an intermediary who ran errands for someone else more powerful than himself. Behind the reserved figure of the doctor must be someone else pulling the strings, someone smarter and more intelligent than he was. Gerd had started to dream about coming into contact with this man. She had always longed to meet a man she could regard as her equal.

"That's all," said Gusov coldly. "You may go now. I want to see Alf Skolle back at work by Thursday at the latest."

He remained seated and did not attempt to offer his hand by way of good-bye. When Gerd rose to her feet, she felt shaky at the knees and was forced to take a deep breath before she could manage to come out with an exit line.

"As you will," she said, but her voice was shrill, the irony weak and blunt.

When Gerd passed by the three businessmen who were still sitting stubbornly on their chairs in the corridor, she had difficulty in forcing a pale smile. If they had not been so preoccupied with their own problems, they might well have got the impression she was about to burst into tears.

Alf Skolle did not reply until the phone rang for the fifth time, and his croaking, almost incomprehensible voice made her realize straightaway he was in an even worse state than she had thought.

"It's Gerd," she said.

"Is that you?" he asked vacantly after a pause of several seconds. His voice expressed no surprise, but begged for sympathy.

"I heard you were unwell."

He muttered some incomprehensible answer, at which point the conversation was interrupted by a bewildering noise, and she eventually realized the phone had fallen on the floor as he got out of bed and dragged it off the bedside table. It was almost half a minute before he managed to pick it up and take hold of the receiver again.

"What do you want?" he asked gruffly, without even attempting to explain away his attitude.

"What you need is someone to look after you," she said softly, and there was no trace of reproach in her voice. "I'm coming round to your place. Is there anything you want me to get for you?"

"A bottle of tin."

It sounded like a sigh of relief.

"God, but my head aches," he went on, sounding perkier already. "If only you knew . . ."

"I do know." She laughed. "But there are better ways of curing the flu. Get ready for a surprise. I'll soon have you on your feet again."

He was muttering away to himself. That was not what he wanted to hear.

"You're welcome when you come," he said quickly, as if he was suddenly afraid he had been too off-putting. "As long as you don't try to put anything over on me."

"I'll never do that again," she assured him quickly. "Neither you nor I can afford to do that. We've got to stick together. If we don't, we could be in trouble."

"What do you mean?"

"I'll be with you in an hour," she said, cutting him off.

Skolle was not particularly worried. Much less than he had been the previous night. He was curious more than anything else. As he stood in the bathroom shortly afterward, he found himself looking forward to it. His experience with women told him it would never occur to them to visit him without having something to offer. He had no doubt at all that they always expected something in return.

9

It would be late Monday afternoon before Herwart Klammer was ready to leave Frey's apartment. Ever since he arrived in Stockholm ten days ago, he had played the role of a disciplined officeworker meticulously observing his working hours. He had risen every morning at half past seven, had a cup of plain coffee, and taken the eight forty-three train to the Underground Central, where he had transferred to a commuter train. Without realizing it, he had always been accompanied by Gudrun Brunhildson. He had never broken his journey, nor had he paused to look round—it seemed as if he were indifferent to whether anyone, friend or foe, was interested in his activities. Klammer behaved like every other wage-slave, and none of the other passengers noticed him, or suspected he might be anything but what he seemed.

Klammer generally returned to the apartment shortly after eleven at night. Gudrun was always within range, although the distance between them was greater at night. It must be said in Klammer's favor that he never called on his landlord at that late hour; so far, he had proved to be a considerate tenant, no trouble at all.

Frey was not surprised when he found Klammer had preferred to stay at home this particular Monday. He had assumed things would change now, and this was one of the reasons why he himself had found something to do in the city early that morning, things which in fact he could very well have left until some other time. He did not want to give the German any indication he knew things were about to change. Frey returned home about the same time the East German plane finally got permission to take off at Arlanda. He puttered around the apartment sufficiently to let Klammer know he was not alone, but he avoided giving any hint that he wanted or expected the other man to join him. The initiative would have to come from the German.

Not a sound had been heard from the Colonel for several weeks now. There was nothing remarkable in that. Their contact was often sporadic and far from regular. There would sometimes be a flat calm lasting for several months. But things were different now, or at least, ought to be. Frey found it difficult to believe the operation he had been ordered to take part in, but about which he knew nothing at all, would be outside the Colonel's control. The few conversations he had had with Klammer had done nothing to help solve the mystery. On the contrary, every time Frey mentioned the Colonel or touched upon subjects and experiences they ought to have in common, Klammer would shut up like a clam. Since that first evening, their contact had been polite but formal, and their conversations had always been about trivialities. Klammer had not said a word about how he was spending these two weeks in wintry Stockholm. On the other hand, he had not asked what Frey was doing with his time either.

Shortly after four o'clock, Klammer came into the living room where Frey was sitting with a glass of beer and the evening paper. Klammer was dressed to go out.

"I think I'll take a walk," he said. "I haven't been out all day, and I need a bit of exercise."

"I'll come with you," responded Frey, getting to his feet. The storm had cleared up, and it was a marvelous winter's day.

"Nice of you to offer, but I've got a few things I want to sort out. On my own. You can think a lot more clearly when you're out in the open air. Don't you think so?"

"You may be right."

"On the other hand," said Klammer, taking a step closer to the table, "I would appreciate it if we could have a little chat this evening. It's about time we talked a few things over. Perhaps we could have a hot punch—I've got a bottle of cognac in my room."

Despite the friendly tone and the offer of a pleasant bit of socializing, it sounded like an order.

Frey nodded.

"I'll be here," he said, and his voice sounded a little sharper than usual.

As the door closed behind the German, Frey stood up and went quickly out into the hall. His expression looked strained. He remained standing in the middle of the floor, grimacing. He had ten seconds in which to make up his mind. It could be vital, and he could not afford to make a mistake.

It was not clear whether Gudrun would have had time to get back from the airport, nor was it clear whether she had decided to continue shadowing Klammer that day. They had both taken it for granted that the German would lie low until everybody connected with the exhibition had left Sweden. At the same time, they had assumed Klammer would decide the time had come for a little talk. Sooner or later he would have to lift the veil a little bit—that is, if he intended to ask for anything specific in the way of help.

That was all perfectly logical, but as always, logical thought was inadequate. The moment Klammer rejected his offer of company, Frey was quite sure he was on his way to a prearranged meeting.

Call it intuition, premonition, or what you like: Frey was certain he was not mistaken despite the fact that he could not actually know, and his certainty was in no way contrary to his logical thinking.

The problem with hasty decisions is that they so often turn out to have been overhasty. Perhaps it was an awareness of that, or the memory of the sorry mess he had made of shadowing Klammer the first day he was in Stockholm, which made up his mind for him. With a sigh, he left his fur coat on its hanger and his winter shoes in the cupboard. He was not prepared to risk another failure. Instead, he went out into the kitchen for a whiskey to salve his annoyance. Somehow or other, he felt he had been outfoxed yet again. He sat there waiting, hoping against hope. If he had been a religious person, one might have said he was bowed in prayer.

Gudrun had a very busy week behind her. Like everybody else, she was in need of food and a good rest. It was not unreasonable to assume she would have decided to go straight home from the airport, that would have been an understandable and logical decision. They had agreed that she would continue tailing the German, but they had also agreed Klammer would most probably not venture out of doors this particular Monday.

Frey always left it to Gudrun to decide how far she should exert herself. At the same time, he was aware that her loyalty and reliability bordered on pigheadedness. What other people would regard as a minor omission or a perfectly acceptable excuse, she would describe as a betrayal. That was the knowledge on which he was basing his meager hopes. If she had not been hampered by the bad weather, there was just a chance Gudrun Brunhildson might be in the vicinity, invisible as always, but alert and determined not to let her prey out of her sight.

The strange thing was that Frey's intuition was reliable with regard to a man like Herwart Klammer, about whom he knew very little in fact, but it was completely inadequate and indeed virtually nonexistent with regard to Gudrun Brunhild-son, whom he had known for over ten years and to whom he was very close. There are human characteristics that cannot be controlled or conjured up, and for which it is difficult to find a logical explanation. Intuition seldom has anything to do with closeness, knowledge, or love. Terror, threats, and fear, on the other hand, can sometimes awaken this base instinct. Not many people are able to detect it, however.

Klammer chose the farthest of the outside doors when he left the building. He remained standing on the pavement for several minutes, as if he were waiting for someone. The traffic had intensified as people were leaving work and driving to their homes in the suburbs, their cars easing their way forward through the slush; the snow had not yet been cleared, so there was only room for one lane. It was a dual carriageway, with a broad row of parked cars down the middle. It was these cars Klammer was scrutinizing, especially the ones that had been swept clear of snow.

Two of the cars had been left with their engines ticking over, and there were several children in the backseat of one of them. Klammer stood there motionless until both the owners had emerged from the grocer's with heavy plastic carrier bags in each hand, and driven away. Only then did Klammer continue his stroll. He was walking away from the underground entrance, down the hill in the direction of the two lakes that were squashed together like two breathing holes in the space between the high-rise blocks of Solna and Sundby-berg. He was not hurrying, but stopped several times and looked around. He was still interested in the parked cars above all else. They were still there, all of them; no one was trying to edge out into the endless stream of determined motorists. Before turning off into the cul-de-sac at the back of the school, he let a fleet-footed young man in a parka go past on his way to the hot dog stall a little way ahead. There was no other pedestrian in either direction for several hundred yards.

The sun was starting to set. Bright red in color, it was flitting in among the trees on the edge of the forest, occasionally peeping out from among the ragged, fast-moving low clouds in the southwest. The storm had passed for now, but that meant the cold air from the north had a clear run and was starting to gobble up lost territory again. It was several degrees colder already. Another twenty minutes and it would be dark, but not pitch dark as the snow reflected the pale light and lit up the road for anyone who was out for a walk. The stars were standing by to take over the lighting duties, and perhaps the moon as well, if it had not set already.

Gudrun was convinced Klammer had been this way before. He took the shortcut through the edge of the woods and did not hesitate at junctions or crossings. That was not why he kept stopping and looking around at regular intervals. At first she was surprised and could not understand how he could have acquired this degree of local knowledge, but then she realized it must have been before she started following him, one of the days shortly after he arrived in Stockholm.

Gudrun had parked her station wagon a considerable distance from Frey's apartment, and taken with her the skis she always kept in the back. After a delayed lunch at Arlanda, she had arrived just five minutes before Klammer appeared in the street. The German's sudden interest in his environment caught her attention immediately, and made her more alert than she had been. His whole manner had changed. The carefree pose he had adopted during the past week, and the many trips out to the exhibition center had vanished, and there was no doubt Klammer was anxious to ensure no one was following him.

The snow was several inches deep on the narrow path

through the woods on the south side of the lake. The ski track was narrow, slippery, and not yet packed down, and it was hard for a pedestrian to walk there. Klammer was not the only one in the neighborhood to appreciate a bracing winter walk. Occasionally he was confronted with a group of yelling, rosy-cheeked youngsters on their way home with their trays and sleds. Gudrun had a much easier task, following behind at a safe distance. From a long way away, no one could distinguish her from the many teenaged girls who had brought out their skis for a few practice runs down the slalom course.

It was even harder for a pedestrian to make progress by the farthest of the two lakes where the terrain was flatter and the wind had piled up the snow in drifts here and there. The occasional adult skier was striding out under the snow-covered oak trees along the edge of the lake, or along one of the two diagonal tracks that had been made across the ice-covered lake.

Gudrun waited for quite some time in the protection of the reeds along one of the short sides of the lake. Now and then she could see Klammer's thin outline among the trees. Not until he had emerged into the open stretch opposite her vantage point and had turned into a shimmering black speck moving slowly through the white landscape almost lacking in perspective did she set off to ski over the frozen lake. When she was about halfway across and Klammer was approaching the wooden bridge, a simple construction that spans the stream of warm water coming from the nearby marshalling yards and, with the help of an artificial waterfall, creates a stretch of open water big enough to accommodate several hundred quacking ducks, she noticed a skier heading across her bows.

She immediately slowed down to ensure that he would pass in front of her. It was a tall man, and she gathered from his slow movements that he was no longer young. They were only a few yards apart when their eyes met for a brief moment; the man stumbled, smiling in embarrassment as he managed to stay on his feet with the aid of his poles. Off he went once more, heading toward the clump of trees on the north bank of the lake.

She had known who he was the moment she saw him, despite the ski outfit and the cap pulled down over his eyes. At the same time, she was sure he had not recognized her. There was no spark of recognition in his eyes, and he could very well have taken her for a fifteen-year-old schoolgirl out skiing to stay in shape.

She was not worried, therefore, when he stopped for a few seconds, leaned on his ski poles, and watched her striding away from him—he just wanted to make sure he would be alone on this side of the lake from now on. The only living creature coming toward him was Herwart Klammer, who had already crossed the bridge and was on his way into the clump of trees.

Without hesitation, Gudrun moved away in the opposite direction, and suddenly seemed to pick up speed, as if she were looking forward to getting home. She had seen all she needed to see. The skier who had crossed her path had visited the East German stand at the fair a few days previously. He had been making an official visit in the company of several other apparently equally important and well-dressed people, and they had been received with enormous respect by their East German hosts. Indeed, they had even cordoned off the stand for a few hours, closing it to other visitors. Gudrun had looked into who the VIP was, and discovered he was one of the Swedes with the most influence on trade between Sweden and the Eastern bloc countries.

Of course, Gudrun could not be certain that the section head at the ministry would enter into a private conversation with Herwart Klammer, but she did not need to know. In intelligence work, as in the legal world, proof is not always necessary. Sufficiently strong circumstantial evidence is enough for probable and sometimes decisive conclusions to be drawn. In any case, Gudrun Brunhildson had managed to nose out a sufficiently important piece of the jigsaw for her to be sure that Frey would have the highest regard for her report of an otherwise uneventful skiing session.

On the way back she paused by the slalom slope, one of the smallest in Sweden where competitions are held but difficult enough to keep the dilettantes at bay. The slope was illuminated, and there was even a lift. Most of the skiers launching themselves fearlessly down the icy slope were children or young people, and they all looked like potential World Cup winners.

It was silly, of course, and perhaps also childish, but she could not resist the temptation. Gudrun Brunhildson had always been a good skier, but that was not why she wanted to take on the slope. She felt extremely pleased with herself, excessively proud, and she was bubbling over with happiness and contentment. A full week of hard work, from early in the morning till late at night, the nervous worry about being outfoxed or exposed, and the hitherto unproductive shadowing of Herwart Klammer had all been worthwhile. She was convinced she had stumbled onto something important. Frey would know exactly where this piece of the jigsaw fit in. It might even enable him to discern the pattern. She was not worried that her discovery could also put her in more danger, that the threat had moved nearer home and that she was also involved now. What was making her feel so good was something quite different. The main thing was she had not failed. Once again, she had managed to live up to the expectations Frey had of her. She smiled wryly. That was unfair. He had no expectations of her. But hopes . . .

She had been lucky, she admitted that freely. Out at the airport she had wondered whether she ought to go straight home. She could do with a good bath and a nice warm room, and she felt she needed to make up for all the lost sleep. It seemed a good opportunity. Out at Sundbyberg, as likely as not, she would have to hang around for hours, for nothing.

Whatever Herwart Klammer was planning to do, caution would push him into staying at home until he was quite certain his namesake had left the country.

Even so, it had gone against the grain. She had felt as if she was about to betray her trust, and in the end, she had made up her mind. Just a few hours, she told herself. You can manage a couple of hours out in the cold all right. If nothing happens by nine o'clock, you can pack up and go home.

From the top, the slope looked more like a precipice, but she just smiled, and did not hesitate for a moment. Maybe she took it a little wider than the others, but even if she did very nearly fall in the depression halfway down, she got to the bottom in one piece, and continued out onto the ice-covered lake at top speed. A broad grin spread over her face, but she had enough sense not to try and do it again. She had collected her reward, and could look back over a successful day. She was more than pleased with herself. She almost danced home.

When she only had the incline leading to the underground station left, she tried to ski past a strange-looking person in a long, ankle-length overcoat. In fact, she had to shout at him before he gave way. As she looked into his immobile but not unfriendly and far from unintelligent face, she thought for a moment she recognized him. She was annoyed with herself. Enough of these suspicions! This man had nothing to do with Herwart Klammer. He probably lived somewhere in the neighborhood—that was no doubt why she had seen him before. She thrust hard on her poles and sped on her way. It was important that she get rid of her skis before the German got back.

She only had to wait half an hour or less. He was on his own, and no longer nearly as worried about what was happening around him. He did not even bother to use one of the alternative entrances, but headed straight for the one leading to Frey's apartment. On his way in, he had to stand aside for two men who were busy clearing the snow outside the door. One of them was the man in the long overcoat. Gudrun could not remember having seen the other one before. He wore a knitted hat on his head, which was spherical in shape, and his smile was as broad and innocent as that of a five-year-old boy whose wish for a pair of new skis had just been granted. The ones leaning against the house wall were no doubt his.

Like Klammer, Gudrun had difficulty in suppressing an amused grin as she watched the hard-working pair.

10

The opposite of intelligence is not stupidity but unawareness. A person with insight knows his insight is limited. He regards every received truth with suspicion, without necessarily rejecting it, and is conscious of the fact that unawareness is rooted in faith or overestimation of oneself.

Whoever had constructed the plan, the cunning manipulator and stage manager who might well be the Colonel but could equally well be someone else, did not have faith. Nor was he an out-and-out cynic, even though ruthlessness must be one of his most striking characteristics. In no sense was he omnipotent. His strength lay in being able to assess people's qualities, and being quite clear about the fact that there is always a limit to how far a person can be pushed before he keels over and becomes completely unreliable. He knew that loyalty is never boundless, and that people can always change, even when they seem to be stuck in their ways.

Needless to say, he was a gambler. He calculated the size of the stake to match the desired winnings, and he took into account coincidence and the unexpected. He must have known Klammer and Frey would never be able to overcome their mistrust of each other, and that as a result, they would make an ideal pair for his purposes. He had divided the right to make decisions between them, and thus made sure neither would let him down.

"I suppose we ought to drink to our shared interests," said Frey, without being quite able to conceal the irony behind his words.

Klammer nodded.

"To our good health," he responded, using a banal German expression.

"Which I assume must mean that somebody or other will suffer."

Klammer looked up, and the sparkle in his eye had nothing to do with reluctance or surprise. He was not entirely without humor.

The tension between them was still there, even if it was no longer noticeable on the surface. Frey smiled a little awkwardly as he raised his cup, which Klammer had first half-filled with tea, then topped up to the brim with Weinbrand. When it came to his own cup, the German had contented himself with a much smaller measure from the fusel-scented bottle.

"You have gathered that," said Klammer, without sounding at all surprised.

"Naturally."

"I know my silence must have surprised you, and maybe even annoyed you," said Klammer meditatively. "To tell you the truth, I have very little to tell you. As you will have gathered, the mission is very important, but you must believe me when I tell you that not even I know all the details. I should add that I have been instructed to avoid involving you in my activities as far as possible."

"But even so, I must be going to take part in a more active way than I have so far. I find it hard to believe the Colonel

103

could not have found somewhere else at least as comfortable as my apartment for you to stay."

"That goes without saying."

Klammer smiled, and Frey could tell from his smile that he knew what was going to come next, what must come next.

"They're given me the right to back out," said Frey.

"True. But you won't do that."

"How can you know that?"

"Because if that were going to happen, they'd have chosen somebody else."

"The Colonel's faith in my loyalty appears to be without bounds," said Frey.

"The Colonel's . . . or the people behind him."

This was the first time Klammer had indicated that they might not have the same master. He must have done it intentionally.

"I think I understand," said Frey, and even though it was not quite true, he had realized immediately that there was a threat behind what the German had said.

We belong to the chosen few," said Klammer all of a sudden.

Frey was astonished, and did not dare look the German in the eye. He had expected anything as far as Klammer was concerned, and was prepared for most things, but not for one moment had he reckoned with such blind faith of almost religious proportions. As he lit a cigarette, he tried to get a glimpse of the German's expression without making it obvious. It was self-assured, but there was no trace of irony. There was no joking, no humor, no wit. Nothing but intense conviction.

"Chosen for what?" asked Frey cautiously.

Klammer smiled a little apologetically and with a touch of self-mockery, as if he had returned to reality after a secret trip to Utopia.

"You know that as well as I do," he replied. "Forgive me if I expressed it a little solemnly—it's the kind of thought one normally keeps to oneself. But if we didn't have them, neither you nor I would be sitting here. We'd be nothing. I'm sure you agree with me, even if you might not put it in quite the same way."

Frey nodded, trying to appear friendly. Then he smiled and hoped the German would construe his smile as confirmation of their shared beliefs. This was the second time Frey had sensed that there were chinks in Klammer's armor after all. The first was when Gudrun had told him about Klammer's off-duty interest in young men. There was a connection here somewhere, but he was not quite sure where.

"I expect to be back in Berlin within a week," said Klammer.

He had an amazing way of changing the subject suddenly and without warning, as if he had suddenly reprimanded himself for being so frivolous and unneccessarily frank. As if it really was time they came to grips with the mission they had both been entrusted with.

"I hope that in the next few days, you can place your services at my disposal."

He had an irritating way of always expressing himself like a bureaucrat. It dawned on Frey that this was exactly what Klammer was. A dutiful bureaucrat in the service of death, faithful to the last paragraph and obedient to the last full stop. He was not lacking in imagination, nor was he short of the ability to act; but even so, he was always ready to do as he was told, always at someone's service. A dangerous man, because he never questioned the intentions of his masters.

"What do you want me to do?"

"Two things. They are linked, and they are of vital importance if I am going to be able to carry out my mission."

Frey said nothing, and waited. He had an idea what was coming, but did not show his unease. At last it would become clear why he had been chosen as Klammer's accomplice.

"We need a car," said Klammer. It was the first time he

had expressed himself in the plural, as if he was assuming that from now on they would be working as a pair.

"It will have to be a fast, reliable car, and I'm afraid you'll have to steal it."

Frey frowned.

"And?"

"We only need it or a few hours on Friday. The later you can acquire it, the better and safer it will be for us. I'm also counting on you to drive with me as passenger."

"Is that all?"

Klammer looked up, and his expression was deadly serious.

"That's all," he replied.

There was one more question to be asked, and just for a second, Frey hesitated to put it. As if he already knew the answer, but would rather not hear it.

"I shall be armed," said Klammer without a moment's hesitation, "and I shall be making use of the weapon."

The subsequent silence was trying for them both. This time it was Klammer who avoided looking Frey in the eye. It is doubtful whether the Swede was aware of what was happening around him. He was staring fixedly ahead, and for the first time in many years Frey felt helpless. He would have liked most of all to run away. But where to? There was no safe haven for him. He did not even have the right to choose freely anymore, despite the fact that this was precisely the exclusive right he had been guaranteed.

"Who's going to be mur . . ."

He did not complete the word. Murder is something your opponents do, or civilians, or criminals. They never did it themselves. They defended themselves as soldiers, or handed out punishment as judges. In extreme cases, they might liquidate a traitor as executioners.

"Who . . . who is it . . . ?" asked Frey.

His voice was hoarse and rasping, and he had trouble in getting out the words.

"Who's going to be . . . ?"

"It would be better for you if you didn't know," answered Klammer.

He looked Frey in the eye, and seemed to be completely calm. It was as if he understood Frey's reaction, or had expected it at least. He leaned over the table and nodded, without trying to assert any feeling of superiority, but not exactly full of compassion either.

"I know," said Klammer. "You need time. We all need time when we're faced with this kind of mission. You don't need to answer immediately, but I need to know by tonight."

Frey looked daggers at the German, who kept his calm and did not seem surprised by the rancour in the Swede's expression.

"I'll let you know in an hour," said Frey, rising demonstratively to his feet, as if he were no longer happy to share his company. He seemed to look straight through the German as he left the room.

It took him over a quarter of an hour before he was ready to leave the apartment. He was not normally a fussy person, but on this occasion it took him quite some time to put on his boots, fur coat, fur hat, and the patterned, knitted gloves he had been given as a Christmas present over a year ago.

Meanwhile, his annoyance—or was it a feeling of helplessness?—had dispersed. He went back into the room where Klammer was sitting hunched up in the armchair, his cognac toddy in front of him.

"Like you, I can think better when I'm on my own," said Frey calmly. "And best of all when I'm plodding through the snow."

There was a trace of a smile somewhere in his grim expression. Perhaps it was no more than a reflection, or a glimmer of unexpressed agreement that shone briefly in Klammer's eyes. There was nothing more to be said for the moment, and so they parted without wasting any more words.

Frey marched down the street at a brisk pace, his mind a blank, until he came to the churchyard between Lötsjön and Hallonbergen. It looked freezing cold and deserted. He had chosen that route partly because he knew most living persons avoided places occupied by the dead during the hours of darkness, and partly because it would take him straight to one of the entrances to the multistory garage in the center of the Hallonbergen complex.

As he closed the heavy churchyard gate behind him and walked past the dignified, white-clad elms at a considerably more thoughtful pace, he seemed to have come back to life again. He felt the paralysis starting to release him from its grip. A paralysis of mind due to the threat, which now at last, after several weeks of nagging, exhaustive waiting, had turned into brutal and ruthless reality.

He was annoyed with himself. The threat had materialized, and he could no longer run away from it. Together with Klammer, he would carry out the mission assigned to them, and then try and escape the subsequent retaliation and persecution. He alone would have to prepare himself for both the car ride with its murderous intent, and his escape once it was over. More worrisome was the fact that he had allowed himself to be led astray by a delusion. They had flattered him by indicating they regarded him as an equal partner. They had sent him a signal of equality, comradeship, and independence, and he had cast aside the mistrust that usually prevented him from being outwitted. But even if he had not allowed himself to be fooled, he would still have been just as bound and restricted as now, just as incapable of escaping from the trap in which he was caught. The difference was that in that case, he would not be reproaching himself like he was now, and that was a burden he must overcome quickly.

In fact, he had not made any conscious decisions. He had not even put up any serious resistance. From the very moment he received the first, cryptic announcement of

Klammer's impending arrival, he had realized but refused to accept that he would be dragged into a mission which would make unpleasant demands on him. The whole time, he had avoided spelling out or even thinking about what the demands might be. He had been hoping for salvation. That was the only word for it. He had harbored faith, and so had begged for mercy; because he had faith, he had been led astray and betrayed.

Someone was going to be killed. Klammer had been picked to hold the weapon, and Frey to drive the car. From a technical point of view, there was no difference, either for the victim or for the judge, with regard to who did what. What worried Frey most, however, was not the obvious risk of failing and being caught, and as a result being condemned to a life sentence. Nor was it his total lack of knowledge about how just or defensible it was to kill this unknown person. The decision had been taken by powerful and sober men, totally lacking in illusions, far away on the other side of the Baltic Sea. Men whose judgment he trusted. Frey had no doubt that these men considered they had good reason to order the liquidation. But there were other worrisome reasons why he had been singled out as an executioner.

If he assumed the unknown person was a potential defector and traitor, and also assumed it was someone close to him who knew about his activities, whoever it was must not only be a threat to him, but also to all his collaborators. In that case it was in Frey's interest, indeed, it was his unashamed duty to ensure that the sentence was carried out ruthlessly. If it came to a choice between himself and somebody else, he would not hesitate.

That could be an explanation of why they had chosen him, why they had kept from him all the details, and why they had sent Klammer to Stockholm. Naturally, close relationships are formed between agents. They do each other favors, they protect each other, and they are dependent on each other. In many respects, the relationship between two

109

agents is more intimate than that between husband and wife. Hence, when someone proves to be treacherous and is unexpectedly transformed into an enemy, it does not mean that all emotional links are severed the moment the suspicion or proof of betrayal is established. Love rarely turns into hatred overnight. Sympathy and trust are not qualities that can be eliminated at a stroke. They crumble and fall apart, sometimes quickly, but never immediately. If the unknown person were someone close to Frey, someone with whom he had worked for a long time, he would first have tried to find out for certain that the accusation was true. Anyone can make a mistake. Proof can be insufficient, or fabricated, or misinterpeted. In any case, there would have been a delay, and Frey would have been held back by understandable hesitation in a situation where quick, ruthless action was essential.

It is always unpleasant, having to accept that someone who has been a friend and comrade is suddenly transformed into a deadly threat to one's own existence. Perhaps that was why they had kept him out of it, and also why they wanted him to take part.

Despite all that is written on the subject, it is rare for intelligence organizations to resort to extreme violence, and not on moral grounds, even though morals are given considerable weight in such circles. It is one thing for an exposed agent to be condemned to death, and then to be executed. That is a case of an opponent punishing his failure. It is quite another matter, however, to expose an agent to a risk that is difficult to control by requiring him to emerge from the shadows and wage open warfare. It does happen even so, and it is always regarded as an outrage by those who are sent out into the merciless sunlight. Frey had reached the Hallonbergen complex, and the garage that covers the whole of its basement. Cars were standing in four rows and on two floors—each apartment was allocated a parking space, irrespective of whether the occupier needed it. It was barely half past five in the evening, but even so, most of the spaces were occupied. Many of the cars still had snow on their roofs, or slush and dirt covered their sides, their license plates crusted over and illegible. But there were also some cars that had quite clearly been put away for the winter, or at least until the streets were clear again. They were not completely clean either, and many had a thick layer of dust showing that they had been there for quite some time, unused.

Frey took his time. He was not alone in the garage, but no one took any notice of him. Every now and then a lone motorist would roll up, or a family coming home with the shopping. All of them hurried straight to the staircases leading up to the apartments. It was impossible to know all one's neighbors by sight here: several thousand people lived in the complex, including a sizable number of immigrants. Nearly everybody had a car, and hardly anyone—apart from the children—mixed with their neighbors.

It is difficult but not impossible to tell from its appearance whether or not a car is in good condition. After wandering through the whole garage, Frey had made his choice. A dark red Volvo in the middle of the center row on the lower floor seemed to be a suitable item for borrowing. The owner had made sure it was thoroughly washed before laying it up for the winter, as well as clearing and cleaning both the front and back seats. This car belonged to an orderly person who looked after his belongings.

Frey had chosen this particular car because its radio was still in place, indicating, he established with a smile, that the owner was not only orderly but also trusting. In all probability, he had also left the battery in the car, without thinking about the possibility of it being stolen. No thieves has been there, in fact: the hood was untouched, and the layer of dust was just as thick on the front of the car as it was on its roof and sides. No one had been near this car for several weeks.

The only thing Frey could not be sure about was whether there was any gas in the tank.

"Thinking of changing your car?"

Frey swung around and found himself looking into Gudrun Brunhildson's smiling eyes, peering out from under her knitted hat.

"You are impossible," he said, relieved to find who had addressed him. He took a step toward her and gave her a hug. It was good she had made her presence known. If anyone had been starting to get suspicious about him after all, any such thoughts would have been dispersed now that it was clear he had been waiting for a woman.

"Completely impossible," he went on. "I was absolutely certain no one was following me. There's at least five hundred yards of open ground between the churchyard and the trees, and I looked around several times. What did you do? Do you use radar?"

"It can sometimes be an advantage, being a little woman. In any case, I'm not going to let you in on any of my trade secrets. Not even you."

"Come on, let's get out of here," said Frey, taking her arm.

They took the elevator up to the ground floor, and looking for all the world like a married couple minding their own business, strolled arm-in-arm along the pavement beneath the power cables, heading for the shopping center.

There were not many adults out in the increasingly bitter cold, but there were plenty of red-cheeked children playing in the snow, not having heeded the urging of their parents to come inside and get warm. They chased each other tirelessly in and out of the snowdrifts, or hurled themselves down the slopes on their sleds or trays. The bravest of them lay on their stomachs, yelling at the top of their voices to warn everyone to get out of their way. None of them paid any attention to a couple of unknown adults plodding through the slush.

"I got here just in time," said Gudrun quietly. "You need a bit of luck sometimes."

Frey stopped abruptly, and from a distance it looked as though they had started an argument.

"You don't mean . . ." he began hesitantly. "Are you telling me you followed Klammer? Just now? About an hour ago?"

"Of course I did."

"And . . . ?"

"He had an appointment. With a man on skis."

She giggled, as if she were teasing him on purpose. But Frey was not in the mood for joking. Not yet.

"So that's why he went out," he said thoughtfully. "I realized it was something important, but I was afraid he might catch me out again if I tried to follow him. And so I stayed at home.

"He was very careful."

"I'm sure he was. But obviously he wasn't clever enough to catch you."

Gudrun laughed out loud, and her satisfaction was audible.

"No," she said. "Not clever enough. On the other hand, the man on skis saw me. Quite close up."

Frey frowned and looked worried.

"You don't mean . . . ?" he asked.

". . . that he recognized me? I'm sure he didn't. You can't remember insignificant little people like me if you yourself are significant. That's an advantage in this job. We've seen each other several times before, though. That's why I know who he is."

Frey did not answer, but once again he took tight hold of her arm; she could feel the tension growing inside him.

"I don't know his name," Gudrun went on.

She was more serious now, but she took her time even

113

so, possibly because she wanted to go on making the most of it. It was her moment of triumph.

"Not yet, at least. But it can't be hard to find out," she said slightly more briskly. "I know what he does: He's a prestigious person. Presumably in a ministry. The East Germans even roped off their stand when he paid them a visit at the fair. That was where I saw him for the first time. Klammer was there as well, but at that time I had no reason to link the two visits. His seemed to be very formal."

"Of course not."

The tone between them now was absolutely serious, as if they both realized they had made a critical discovery.

"You said you'd seen him on some other occasion, didn't you?" asked Frey.

"That was at the cocktail party at the exhibition center. The manager fussed around him as if he were one of the VIPs."

"A politician?"

"Hardly. But he could be a high official. Even the minister treated him like an equal."

They had got as far as the stairs leading down to the shopping center, and continued in silence for a short while.

"I don't know what it means," said Frey, "but I know it's significant."

Gudrun nodded in agreement.

"Do you want me to find out who he is?"

"Do you think you can do that by tomorrow night?"

"Of course."

"I'll come round to your place at eight o'clock or so. Try and catch up on your sleep, if you can. You needn't worry about Herwart Klammer tomorrow. I'll be having a chat with him shortly, a sort of information session. Even though I'm sure he won't say a word about any man on skis."

"Don't keep him waiting. He's a suspicious type, although I can guarantee he's still at home in your apartment."

114

Frey leaned forward and kissed her on the mouth. It was a cool kiss, like feeling a touch of frost on your lips.

"I don't suppose you're going the same way as me, are you?" he asked with a smile.

"Not just now at least."

"I'll bet you anything I'll never know in any case," said Frey.

11

Most Europeans west and north of the Oder probably find it a little difficult to envisage what a contemporary Soviet citizen means when he talks of an "orgy." The time is long since gone when the depraved Russian upper classes would satisfy their desires to the melancholy accompaniment of balalaikas and sensuous gypsy dancing girls. The wild drinking parties, duels, and gambling sessions, when a thousand souls could swap masters overnight, are no more. Whatever goes on nowadays takes place in private, and on the surface, everything looks so puritanical and woefully boring. Nevertheless, a country that counts a Prince Potemkin among its heroes should never be underestimated.

All the same, it must be even more difficult to imagine what the dry-as-dust brochure-hunter, Dr. Dimitri Gusov, had in mind when he urged Gerd Angerbo to set up an orgy. A small-scale orgy, it is true, but even so.

It had never occurred to any Swede who had ever come across Dr. Gusov, and most probably none of his fellow-countrymen either, that he might had a love life. People jump so easily to false conclusions. Everywhere, there are men and women falsely accused of being sexless. Dimitri Gusov was not the type to collect sexual adventures, but there again, he was not ignorant of the subject, nor was he uninterested in the sexual behavior of humans. His own personal experience was rather limited and by no means remarkable. This was largely due to the petty bourgeois life-style the middle grade of Soviet officialdom was supposed to adhere to. When he was abroad, he was always afraid a little adventure might well have been set up by the opposition. Like all Russians, he overestimated the conspiratorial abilities of the CIA and MI6, not to mention SÄPO. As a result, Dr. Gusov was celibate during his tour of duty in Stockholm. Even so, he had no scruples when it came to dicing with other peoples urges, having attended several KGB courses on the subject; it must be admitted that the top grade course at least was quite advanced.

According to the textbook, psychological stress can often be cured by uninhibited sex. Hence Dr. Gusov instructed Gerd Angerbo to avail herself of this method of leading Alf Skolle into a different and more appropriate way of thinking. The Russian was convinced his diagnosis was correct. Skolle would find a spell in bed would cure him of his simulated influenza, and as a result, he would be able to return to work at the ministry straight-away.

The orgy never took place. Not because Gerd Angerbo lacked the talent or desire to partake in such activities—she had never been afraid of men. On the contrary, she was fascinated by the many-sided nature of the male species. There was a time when she preferred casual affairs, and she used to make sure such opportunities occurred at frequent intervals. Her sensuality had not been satiated with the passing years, and now she had reached the age where some women begin to fear they might soon be burnt out. She still had not experienced anything she herself would describe as orgiastic. She would occasionally daydream about an unin-

117

hibited, passionate, wild orgy in which she was always joined by a number of men. She longed for ecstasy of that sort, but she had never quite managed to achieve it. Perhaps she was incapable of appreciating that the biggest obstacle was her own conceit.

Alf Skolle had no place in her dreams. His performance in bed in no way measured up to the expectations a mature woman might reasonably apply to his attractive appearance and masculine aura. When Alf Skolle peeled off his elegant outer layer, he also removed a portion of his manliness. All that remained was a decidedly ordinary presence that, to crown it all, had great difficulty in keeping awake.

When Gerd Angerbo arrived in Alf Skolle's apartment, she did not come in the guise of a courtesan or mistress. Instead, her demeanor was that of a nurse determined to mother him. Skolle was in a deplorable state, and did not even bother to make an effort. She had never seen him so depressed, so utterly naked. It is true he had opened his heart to her in the past, and there were many weaknesses she had difficulty forgiving him for. The causes could always be traced back to his drinking, but explanations do not always lead to sympathy, and even less often to forgiveness.

He was dirty and unshaven. His face was covered with stubble. It was reddish, and several days old. The bags under his eyes were half-full and flabby, as if they had at last started to be drained of the flood of distilled liquid he had consumed during the last few days. His eyes were watery and blood-shot, and he had difficulty in keeping his head erect. Alf Skolle in fact displayed all the despicable signs of a drunkard on an early retirement pension.

What horrified her most was his eyes. Although they featured a whole spectrum of colors, they were as lifeless and turgid as a muddy pool. He seemed to be squinting, as if he had lost contact with the real world. At first, she was not even sure he knew who she was. He stared at her as if she were a ghost, and did not utter a word of greeting. Then he muttered something incomprehensible, gestured awkwardly with his head, and returned to the living room.

She was quite sure about what was wrong. There was no doubt Skolle was scared, almost paralyzed by fear. Not just worried or uneasy, not just hung over and maudlin, but possessed by the kind of terror that can threaten to choke a man when he is forced to acknowledge he is finished, and there is no hope left.

Gerd paused a little in the hall, trying to shake off a strange and unpleasant feeling of having just looked into a mirror. Of seeing her own fear reflected in Skolle's bleary eyes. She had spent the last hour trying to run away from herself and her own angst, refusing to think about the threat implied by Dimitri Gusov's changed and frightening behavior. She suddenly realized the threat was not directed at her alone, but that she must share it with Alf Skolle.

She sighed, loudly and audibly, as she peeled off her outer clothes, but it was not a sigh of resignation or helplessness. She was not cowed yet. As she adjusted her makeup in the hall mirror, her expression became sharper and her eyes steelier. At length, she gazed boldly at her own reflection and nodded resolutely. The Russian had succeeded in shaking her, that was true, but she was not beaten. She took another deep breath and decided her temporary weakness was now a thing of the past.

Gerd donned her most winning smile as she entered the room where Skolle slouched back like a knocked-out boxer in one of the armchairs. She stood in front of him, waiting for him to open his eyes so she could be sure he would understand what she was saying. Then she laid her cool hand gently on his brow; stroked his lank, sweaty, blond hair; and started massaging his neck.

"No, my friend," she whispered in his ear, "let's make a man of you."

He muttered something inaudible, and it was difficult to

119

decide whether it was in protest or agreement. It made no difference. She was already sure of succeeding.

Skolle was asleep, and when she looked at him she could see he was smiling in his slumbers. Like a naughty little boy. She had bathed him, and shaved him, sitting on a stool beside the bath. Then she had dried him and rubbed him down and wrapped him in a big, white bath towel. When he threw that off in the bedroom, she could see the warmth and massage had done him good. Alf Skolle was usable, for the moment at least. She had kissed him, first his ears and then his mouth. She had sunk slowly to her knees, taken hold of his stiff penis and pecked at it with her tongue, like a little bird. She had finished off with a wet, sucking kiss and he, legs apart like a cavalry major, had tensed his thighs and calves, and trembled with desire.

She had tipped him hastily into the disheveled bed, where the covers and pillows resembled a roller coaster in miniature. She did not want him failing to rise to the occasion, and hence resisted her immediate urge to make it all a little more pleasant by making the bed and smoothing down the sheets. He did not notice how she turned her nose up on catching a whiff of the stale smell from the rumpled sheets, which were liberally sprinkled with dirty brown stains. His eyes were screwed up, and it was quite different parts of her body that held his attention now. Eagerly and attentively, he watched her getting undressed.

She did not make a big fuss about it, but took advantage of the dimmer light in the far corner of the bedroom. He had raised himself up on one elbow, and occasionally caught a glimpse of her naked breasts. As she peeled off her tight-fitting stockings, she turned away from him and stuck out her bottom, so that he could enjoy the shadow-play in the half light. Her naked pink buttocks danced up and down in wave like movements, and he licked his lips in anticipation. The whole operation took only a minute and a half, then she

120

turned to face him, displaying her femininity in its full frontal splendor. He moved over contentedly as she crept into bed beside him and begged him to satisfy her immediately.

It was hardly an orgy.

One of Gerd Angerbo's most fundamental characteristics was her need to keep everything neat and tidy. When she became very formal and spoke about herself in high-sounding but also conceited terms, she used to maintain that what she set most store by in this world was—honesty. It always impressed her listeners, who found it difficult to object; no one wanted to give the impression of being iniquitous or perfidious. What was meant by honesty in a philosophical sense was something Gerd had never really established. She simply lacked all the necessary qualifications for distinguishing between right and wrong. She was unusually well endowed by nature to be an egoist, and her moral views were self-serving. Anything useful to her was good. If anyone placed obstacles in her path, they had to be removed.

Frey's characterization of Gerd Angerbo was appropriate and came very close to the truth: She was a human chameleon. It would never occur to her knowingly to break the law in her role as a citizen. She paid her taxes on time, seldom received a parking ticket, and was scrupulously honest in filling out her tax declaration. Only once had she received an official brown envelope from the tax people demanding unpaid dues, and that was the result of an oversight that could be put right immediately—the trivial incident unsettled her even so. She had acquired a blot on her reputation as a citizen, one that could never be washed away. When she told Frey what had happened and he tried to dismiss the whole business with a joke, she was most upset. It took him a long time to restore good relations. You just did not make fun of things as serious as a demand note from the authorities.

Gerd had nothing but contempt for petty theft, and if the cashier in the supermarket made an error in her favor, she always made sure it was put right. She would have felt mean and unworthy if she had kept the money. At the same time, she was quite capable of planning a meeting with one of her agents in Swedish industry who would supply her with sensitive technical information and thus commit larceny, turning her into a fence and perhaps even a traitor. It never occurred to her that her secret activities could be immoral or criminal. She knew what she did was punishable, and so it must be kept secret and people must not know about it. As long as her secret was not exposed, she felt no qualms of conscience.

In many respects, Gerd Angerbo was a very bourgeois person. She got up at exactly seven o'clock every morning, had her nutritious breakfast, and started to plan her day. She never missed a meeting or forgot to take a telephone call. No one could accuse her of being careless, lax, or unreliable, perhaps that very fact was her greatest weakness. She was very dependent on what others thought about her. Even a joking reprimand could make her feel depressed and worried. She found it easy to exaggerate other people's interest in herself, and she hated reproach as much as she loved praise. The praise should ideally be unelaborated and made known to a wide range of people, so that she could preen herself and display all the likableness and generosity she dreamed of being known for.

There were jealous or perceptive people who thought Gerd Angerbo was an ingratiating person. No one doubted her intelligence or ambition, but people sometimes smiled at her behind her back. She sometimes went too far and could be excessively fussy. An agent could not wish for a better mask. If anyone had suggested Gerd Angerbo was a secret agent in addition to carrying out her normal duties as a citizen, they would have been laughed out of court. She was far too interested in attracting attention to herself. Besides, her job involved spreading information, not keeping it secret.

* * *

At ten o'clock the next morning, Alf Skolle was still asleep. To her relief, he had left her in peace the whole night and evidently had no difficulty in reconciling himself to the fact that she preferred to sleep alone on the living room sofa. Now it was time to put a bit of life into him.

Gerd had used her free morning to analyze her own situation, and also their joint one. She had concluded that, for the moment at least, they were both in the same boat, and they would have to reef the sail. The situation was not hopeless—she would never admit that, neither to him nor to herself. It was difficult to control, however, and to survey. It was essential that they worked together closely and purposefully. On her terms, of course. She had worked out a plan designed to save them both. There was a way of escaping from the trap Dimitri Gusov had enticed them into , and after a few hours' thought, she was convinced she had found the right solution. All that was needed now was to convince Alf Skolle there was no other way out.

The breakfast tray was set on the kitchen table. There are few acts of love in this world to compare with the feeling of pampered luxury bestowed by being woken up by a smiling face serving the first meal of the day the moment one opens one's eyes. It only remained for the coffee percolator and toaster to signal that they were ready. It was during these idle moments that she was suddenly stricken by her orderly conscience. Even if no one would miss her at the exhibition center today, it was safest—to cover all eventualities—to let them know where she could be contacted.

"It's a good thing you rang," announced the operator.

Her indifferent, nasal voice was even more nasal at this time in the morning, if that is possible, and suggested she was disappointed rather than relieved that the call had been made. Gerd had always disapproved of the way the switchboard girl conducted herself. It suggested a lax approach.

123

"The Russian. Gusov. You know. He rang five minutes ago."

"What did he want?"

"He'll be here at eleven rather than twelve, which was the time you'd agreed.

Gerd gasped for breath and gave vent to a noise that was halfway between a sigh and a curse. They had not agreed to meet today at all. Dimitri Gusov had simply taken a chance and she was not sure whether she ought to congratulate herself, or curse the impulse that had made her ring.

"Damned Russians!" she said, tight-lipped. "I'll take a taxi. Bang goes my solarium appointment."

As she replaced the receiver she was sure she could hear a masochistic giggle at the other end of the line. Those two would never be able to get on together.

"I've been a right idiot," said Gerd to Alf Skolle's astonishment, after waking him with a kiss and putting the breakfast tray on the bedside table.

"It's too early for such confessions," he replied, sleepy but contented. "I thought we agreed I was the one who provides all the idiocy."

"Not always. If I hadn't rung the exhibition center to ease my guilty conscience, I could have stayed here with you all day. As it is, I have to disappear for a few hours. But I'll be back by one or so."

"Duty calls, I suppose."

"No. But the exhibition manager does."

"Bosses are a curse, and always will be. They are incapable of understanding that one's private life comes first."

"You're so right."

"I've got nothing against a few hours to myself," said Skolle, and there was something in his voice that suggested he had made up his mind to get a grip on himself.

"By the time you get back, you'll find a new and

improved Alf Skolle," he assured her. "I'll have put my outward appearance to rights at least."

"That won't be good enough," she replied gently. "We're going to have to be strong. That goes for both of us."

He glanced quickly at her. She could see his restlessness was returning, and his wandering eyes betrayed his insecurity.

"Then we'll need something to build our strength up," he muttered, as if searching for something to hide behind.

"Will you bring something back?"

She frowned, and her eyes grew stern. He realized she was about to lose her temper. He didn't want that at all. No rows, no idiotic confrontations. Everything had gone so well so far this morning.

"You don't need to worry," he quickly assured her, trying to sound convincing. He had regretted his request almost before it had crossed his lips. "A bottle of wine will be fine," he said, trying to put things right by giving her his most charming smile. "The best you can get," he went on. "From now on, I intend my relationship with alcohol to be on the most exclusive of levels."

She hesitated, thought for a moment, then gave way. Her curt nod indicated she was prepared to deviate marginally from the hard line she had laid down for the pair of them.

"We have a lot to talk about," she said, stroking his hair. "Today's the day we really start getting to know each other."

She was unsure and did not really know where she had him. She returned to the living room once more to check, letting the taxi wait. Skolle got out of bed. Dressed in his elegant dressing gown, he was standing with his hands in his pockets, gazing out into the dazzling white neighborhood. A pale sun was struggling to break through the clouds, and it was snowing as usual this winter. Fairlike clouds of powdery snow were dancing down toward the streets of Stockholm.

Skolle turned slowly when he heard her coming. His expression was thoughtful, and he looked tired. When she went up to him and put her fur-clad arm around his shoulders, he smiled a little doubtfully at first, then inclined his head and allowed himself to be consoled by the soft, downy sleeve caressing his cheeks.

"You must promise me one thing," said Gerd solicitously. "You must stay here till I get back. It's very, very important. It could be crucial for both of us."

Just for a moment, he looked as helpless as a little child, uncomprehending; she had given no hint at all as to what was threatening them. Then he drew himself up and moved away from her. It was as if he had realized he could no longer wallow in self-pity and had to pull himself together, be strong and self-confident. His expression stiffened and became solemn. He had suddenly aged by ten years. He looked grown-up. Perhaps she had managed to make a man of him at last.

"I won't run away," he said morosely. "In any case, there's nowhere I could hide."

"That's my man!" Gerd sounded consoling. "I'm relying on you."

She had no other choice.

Dr. Gusov was waiting in the reception area when Gerd arrived at the exhibition hall a couple of minutes past eleven. The manager had emerged from his office to greet the Russian, who had explained politely that he was just making a fleeting visit to sort out a routine matter. He was interested in getting hold of some figures regarding the fair that had just finished, information he needed for the final report his superiors in Moscow were waiting eagerly for. Gerd Angerbo had been kind enough to put herself at his disposal.

"We're always at your service," said the manager, looking pleased. "Never hesitate to ask us for help—that's what we're here for. As far as I can judge, your taking part in the fair must have been a considerable success for your export industry. Several people have told me that."

126

Gusov bowed politely and assured him that that was his impression as well.

Smiling broadly, the manager withdrew to his luxurious office. He was an experienced professional and never forgot to compliment a foreign participant. He nearly always managed to squeeze out of them a polite comment agreeing with his assertions, which he would then pass on in confidence to other important exhibitors, and preferably journalists, now ascribing the original statement to the foreign spokesman. As in all branches of marketing, it was essential to embroider facts and present them in as favorable a light as possible, without too much regard for the truth.

On the other hand, it never occurred to the exhibition manager that Dr. Gusov could have obtained the information he wanted in a much simpler way, without putting himself to any trouble. A phone call to Gerd Angerbo would have been quite sufficient. When it came down to the crunch, there was not much to add to what had been provided in the press handouts. In any case, the latest figures had been published in the newspapers that very morning.

The old-fashioned chivalrous and almost servile manner in which Gusov welcomed Gerd Angerbo when she arrived at the exhibition center a few minutes late was dropped and transformed into brusqueness the moment they entered her office. Without saying a word, he closed the door behind them, checked to make sure the intercom was switched off, and looked for a moment as if he were contemplating going over the whole room in a search for bugging devices. Reluctantly, he desisted from such an inspection and instead pointed to the chair on the other side of Gerd's desk.

"There!" he said sternly.

He himself sat on the visitor's chair, his back ramrod straight, his mouth clamped in a grimace of annoyance.

"Make sure we're not interrupted," he said curtly.

Gerd did as she was bidden, trying to control her nervousness and smiling meekly. It had no effect on the

Russian, who stared fixedly back at her. He said nothing and displayed not a trace of humor. She tried hard to meet his gaze without showing any fear, and blushed slightly on discovering that her knees were beginning to shake. She gritted her teeth and choked back her smile, hoping he would not notice anything.

"How's Skolle?"

"He's . . . better," Gerd answered.

It sounded silly, even to her.

"He must be back at work tomorrow." That was an order, and brooked no contradiction or protest. "You did as I suggested?"

He looked at her like a schoolmaster waiting for one of his pupils to answer and confirm the statement he had just made.

She nodded sullenly. If he expected her to blush, he was mistaken.

"I knew that was the right treatment," said Gusov, chuckling with satisfaction. "People here in the West have never managed to shake themselves free from the biological scourge."

Gusov seemed very pleased with his turn of words, even if his maxim was doubtful to say the least, both from a philosophical and an ideological point of view. Suddenly and unexpectedly, he had once again changed his manner toward her. Perhaps it was the confirmation that she had obediently carried out his orders which helped to change his mood. Or perhaps it was just part of the game he was playing in order to get her where he wanted her.

Deep down, they were quite similar. Now he seemed to be confidential, almost friendly, and he even smiled at her as he leaned over the desk. They were both human chameleons.

"Alf Skolle must be back at work tomorrow," reiterated Gusov in a low voice.

Over and over again he was stressing that Skolle must be

back in the ministry without delay. Gerd was suspicious and of two minds. Had she misjudged him?

"The day after tomorrow, at the very latest, his minister will receive a top secret document drawn up by the men at the very heart of the Swedish government and distributed only to a very small number of people. It's about the redrawing of borders between our countries in the Baltic Sea, and spells out the various positions your government will take. The matter will be taken up when your prime minister visits Moscow in a few months."

Gerd was dismayed, and just for a moment was panic-stricken. What she really wanted to do was to stand up and yell straight out that she wanted no more to do with all this, but she managed to control herself. She had miscalculated. That morning she had imagined it would be weeks, perhaps even months before Gusov again started making demands on her and Skolle. That would have given them time to carry out the plan for breaking free that she had worked out. After all, it was no more than ten days since she had handed over the Polish papers and Dr. Gusov had expressed his satisfaction with their efforts. His threatening behavior had come as a surprise to her, but when she had got over the fear she had felt at first, she had found a reasonable explanation. The Russian was planning one last job for them, and hence, naturally, it was extremely important that Alf Skolle should be kept in good shape and should not neglect his work. "Come next spring, you can find yourself a new lover." That was how he had put it at the cocktail party, and it had led her to believe they had several months before anything crucial was going to happen.

"Alf Skolle is certainly in better shape today than he was yesterday," she said, licking her lips, "but I'm not sure whether he's well enough to take on a new mission already."

Gusov smiled maliciously. A good agent never leaps at the prospect of a new mission. Like Gerd, most of her type of agent respond by making a series of objections or easily mumbled excuses. It is all part of their negotiating technique, and paradoxically, it soon builds up their self-confidence. Difficulties are dragged up and distorted, but smoothed over by the contact man. The risks are exaggerated or overstated, but reduced to size logically by the negotiating partner. Really, what they would all prefer to do is to lie low and keep in the shadows. It is safest there, but the idleness and lack of tension can also be a strain. Some of them claim they regard their previous activities as a closed book that they have managed to put clean out of their minds. Nearly everything they say is untrue. The contact man then has to pander to their greed and make a bid he knows is too low, which is then increased bit by bit until it reaches a point where the agent is convinced he is one who has won. He never does. In more difficult cases the only alternative is blackmail or threats. This method is the surest of all, but it presumes you have enough firm ground to stand on and the agent knows the threats will be carried out forthwith.

A third method is to take your opponent by surprise, and this is what Dr. Gusov intended doing.

When an agent exaggerate the dangers and claims to be afraid of a new mission, this is not a sign of weakness or a lack of competence. On the contrary! It shows he is aware of the risks and that he will do all he can to protect himself—and in so doing, ensure that the mission will be successfully completed. There are people who seek out adventure for adventure's sake, but they do not usually last long in this peculiar job. Such types are occasionally recruited, but only for odd missions that are either so risky or hopeless that no intelligence officer in the world would dream of exposing one of his own men to what he would regard as a suicide mission. Even the humblest of agents are too valuable and too difficult to recruit to be risked in a game of chance when the odds are stacked against them. After all, even such an agent represents a significant capital investment and every sensible secret service must be careful with its resources.

Gerd's objection thus did not come as a shock to Gusov. He had expected her to be awkward. The problem was, they were short of time. In lots of ways. And so he had decided to use the surprise method.

"A hundred and fifty thousand kroner," he said calmly.

It was a bombshell.

"A hundred and fifty thousand kronor," he said again, to make sure she had both heard and understood.

Gerd was amazed. She looked nonplussed and sat there for a few seconds with her mouth wide open, unable to come out with a single word. It was a prodigious amount, more than she and Alf Skolle combined would normally be paid for their services, over a full year.

"Wh . . . when?" she stammered, confused.

"When you hand over the goods," answered the Russian, showing no sign of emotion. Deep down, all he felt was contempt.

"What day will that be?"

"Probably this Friday."

She needed breathing space in order to get a grip on herself and start thinking clearly. Gusov had lit a cigarette and was lounging back in his chair. His self-satisfied expression annoyed her.

"Take your time," he said. His voice was friendly.

She was tempted by the money. She always was. Her bank balance was not inconsiderable, and that very morning it had been by no means easy for her to decide to use some of her own money to free both herself and Alf Skolle from Gusov's clutches. She could not count on any help from Skolle—he owned nothing apart from his apartment, and had plenty of debts. Gusov's hundred and fifty thousand kronor were like pennies from heaven.

It was the money that made her mind up for her. The Russian would get his way on this occasion as well. But it would be the very last time.

Gerd was not insensitive to possible danger. Her intuition was often spoiled by her self-assurance, but in critical circumstances she will still able to hear when the alarm bells started ringing. Yesterday the Russian had threatened her and bared his teeth. Today he was as meek as a lamb and was promising her and Alf Skolle a little fortune. There was something about this mission that did not quite add up. Gusov had always maintained that one could never be too cautious. Nothing should be overhasty or spontaneous, everything should be meticulously planned in detail. It would sometimes be several weeks, a month even, before he declared himself satisfied with their arrangements.

"Why are we so short of time?" demanded Gerd. "Why this rush?"

Dr. Gusov was ready for the question.

"Sometimes one has to break rules that are golden ones under normal circumstances," he said calmly. "Do you want to hear my justification?"

She nodded expectantly.

"Our information is only a couple of days old. As I said, the decision was made by the inner cabinet, and it has been shrouded in secrecy. The document will only be at the ministry for a few hours. It will be sent for the minister's information, and they will ask him to comment on the consequences of a negative outcome for trade between our two countries. We don't know exactly when the document will be sent, neither day nor time, but it will probably be this Friday. That means Alf Skolle must be back at work by tomorrow."

"How can you be so sure he will be involved at all?"

Gusov looked at her reproachfully.

"You know as well as I do," he said wearily, "that the minister has only two confidants in the whole ministry, and Alf Skolle is one of them."

Gerd nodded. It was true. Skolle had managed to make himself indispensable to his boss. Sometimes she thought it was a mystery why that should be. He must be quite different at work from what he was in his private life.

The explanation was satisfactory. But how would they be able to steal the information?

."If the document is as secret as that, you can be sure Skolle won't be left alone with it," she said.

"We don't know that," countered Gusov. "It's possible. If not, he'll have to give us a written summary of the contents."

For the second time in a short while Gerd was astonished.

"But in that case the reward would be reduced to fifteen thousand kronor," added the Russian coldly.

Never before had Gusov been prepared to accept an oral report or a written summary of information he was interested in obtaining. On the contrary, he had always insisted on photocopies of the original. "Anything short of that is useless—anybody with a bit of imagination could have made it up," he used to say. This was the first time he had ever deviated from that rule. The secret document must be of exceptionally great importance to the Russians.

At the same time, she had been given an explanation for Gusov's surprising generosity. It was a decoy, but much too obvious for her not to realize that. Of course it was inconceivable that Skolle would have an opportunity of photographing it. Even if he was very handy with a camera. Or . . .

"I understand," said Gerd. Her tone of voice was now as cool as Gusov's.

Without warning Gusov started talking about the fair—that little bit of business was sorted out in a matter of minutes. Gerd escorted him politely to the reception area and helped him on with his overcoat. The exhibition manager emerged from his office again.

"I trust you have received the information you need," he said with a friendly smile.

"Your information officer has been extremely helpful,"

replied Dr. Gusov politely. "I'm afraid I'm a nuisance, but I've asked Miss Angerbo for a little more data, which she has promised to get for me by tomorrow."

"You're always very welcome," said the manager. "It's a pleasure to do whatever we can for you."

As Dr. Gusov left, it occurred to the manager that it was the first time he had ever seen the Russian without his bulky briefcase.

12

Jonas Mikael Frey felt put out and unfairly treated. They had degraded him and turned him into a secondary figure. Klammer had come to Stockholm in order to kill somebody, and they had picked Frey right from the start to be his accomplice, his driver. That was all. They had played their crafty games and tricked him into a position from which he could no longer extract himself. He was in a cul-de-sac, and the only exit was barred. They had taken advantage of his vanity, his loyalty, and his naïveté. As usual, there was no limit to their capacity to manipulate things.

He had always thought of himself as a harbinger of peace. It certain parts of the world that was an honorable title. It implied a person had a certain standing and was prepared to risk his own freedom for the sake of a global cause that would save the world from misery, poverty, and bestiality. Now they had turned him into a henchman of death.

It was not the moral side of the business that worried him most—every day, all over the world, people who had usurped power issued instructions to wipe out other people. These death sentences, whether they were secret or public, were always justified and defended in the same way: The social order must be protected. The right to preserve and lead one's own life must not be questioned. The free world must be protected from the Communist plague, or, the achievements of socialism must be defended. The people of this world are crying out for freedom from exploitation and oppression.

All sides agree the ends justify the means. This is the jesuitic and constantly evoked dogma of Christianity that is paradoxically opposed to Christian beliefs. In the Muslim world they arm themselves for holy war. Others have expressed themselves in a more popular and folksy way, and not all of them were Christians. "Revolutions are not made with rosewater." "Better dead than red." "Freedom is a noble thing. . . ." There is no end to the empty phrases.

Somebody has to carry out the sentences. Someone must wield the axe or pull the trigger. The young are won over by lofty sentiments and rousing oratory; they kill for the sake of the paradise to come. Others are compelled by threats or extortion to become avengers. A few are quite simply bought for a sum of money.

The executioner has always been feared, but never respected. The halos of soldiers begin to fade the moment the last echo from the trumpets at the victory parade has died away. If a warrior has been defeated, he is treated like an outcast and onlookers feel ashamed at the very sight of him. A secret agent, the armor-bearer of silent warfare, is perhaps hated more than anyone else—especially by those he has outwitted and deceived. In their eyes, he represents a contemptuous question mark against their own excellence, an abscess on the legal and social order that only they have the right to control. Even so, a secret agent is rarely honored by the people who have gained from his efforts.

The root of Frey's dissatisfaction was his being made nothing more than a tool. A henchman. He considered himself too valuable to be exposed to the risk involved in taking part in a premeditated murder. He had overestimated himself, and was aware of it; in the eyes of those making the decisions, he was no more than a pawn to be moved around at will. Nevertheless, he did not doubt for a moment that the deed was justified, or at least well founded. The whole business, the secrecy surrounding Klammer's arrival and stay in Stockholm, suggested the mission was of the greatest possible importance. What made Frey so dejected was not fading loyalty or repressed fear; the cause was quite different. He felt offended because he had been downgraded.

"I find it difficult to accept that they have treated me like this," said Frey.

"You can still get out," countered Gudrun Brunhildson. "The Colonel gave you the signal. The sign of equality."

"Not now I can't," he said. "It's too late. If I withdraw now, that would be treachery, and you know what the punishment is for that. Klammer has told me why he has come here. He's revealed his plans to me—partially at least. When he pointed out the Colonel had given me the right to make my own mind up, as you just did, it was no more than a polite gesture on his part."

He shook his head, as if she had mentioned something preposterous.

"In this job, there's no room for defectors," he said. "Nor witnesses. Just accomplices."

Frey had told her the whole story, or, rather, what little he knew or thought he knew and had kept from her so far. She had listened, solemnly and thoughtfully, without interrupting and with no sign of emotion. She had not uttered a single word of complaint about his previous silence.

"I'm also a witness," she said with a smile. "You've made me one."

He looked up, irritated, as if she had reprimanded him.

"That's true," he said peevishly. "But not in the same way."

"What's the difference?"

"The difference," he muttered gruffly, with a frown, "is that I'm not Klammer. I would never hurt you."

"Maybe not," she said. There was a trace of a wry smile on her lips, and an ironic glint in her eye.

She took hold of his hand, forcing him to look her in the eye.

"I know how it is," she said tenderly. "I believe you. But the difference between you and me in this connection—if there is one—is quite simply that Klammer does not know of my existence. I'm an invisible witness. Let's hope so, at any rate. For your sake as well as mine."

He sighed.

"You're right," he said.

They sat in silence for a while, lost in thought.

"So it's Friday is it . . . that's when . . . it'll happen."

"I think so."

"He respects you."

"What do you mean?"

"In a way, he must have enormous confidence in you."

"Confidence?"

"Either he doesn't want to or he can't reveal the background to this mission. It's possible he doesn't know the whole story himself. They might well be manipulating him just as much as you. He knows your qualifications, and when they picked you to be his accomplice, he knew you were the best man there was. In every way."

"You've changed sides," he said in annoyance. "I've had enough of your flattery. It's my damned vanity that's got me into this mess to start with."

Gudrun roared with laughter, and he was forced to smile in return.

"Not vanity," she said in amusement. "Something much more serious. Hurt pride. I've had experience of that, and I know what it can lead to."

There was another pause. Being silent together can sometimes be a good thing.

138

"Those damned German swine," growled Frey in annoyance.

There was no doubt he meant every word.

"A racist insult, but a correct description," said Gudrun, agreeing with him.

Her harsh tone of voice made it clear there was good reason to take her comment at face value.

"From now on, I'll manage on my own," he said, his voice serious. "It's not for me to expose you to any more risks. It's going to be war, and, strictly speaking, it's a war that has nothing to do with you."

"Come off it!"

"I mean it."

"Jonas," said Gudrun, and there was something protective in her voice. "You'll need me more than ever these next forty-eight hours."

"Why?"

She smiled indulgently.

"What is it you usually say? To go on being your invisible eye, of course. So that you know what's in store for you."

He made no reply, nor did he attempt to come out with any more protests; he knew she was right. It was clear she had no intention of continuing a conversation when they both knew how it would end up, and hence it was pointless.

They were in her apartment, drinking coffee. It was still not half past eight in the morning. She had shown no trace of surprise when she opened the door an hour earlier and found him standing there. She was already fully dressed, and he immediately had the impression she had been expecting him.

Half an hour later, Frey was having his second cup of coffee that morning, only now it was in his own kitchen. Klammer was with him.

"You were up early today," said the German, who had been there long enough to know Frey's normal habits.

He rarely left the apartment before eleven in the morning, and Klammer usually saw him in his dressing gown when he left for the exhibition center.

"I wanted to scout around a bit," said Frey cautiously.

The German looked up. It was difficult to know if he was suspicious, or just curious.

"Scout around?"

"The car."

"Of course. Have you found anything suitable?"

Frey nodded.

"It's in a garage less than a quarter of an hour's walk from here, and no more than eight minutes by car. It'll be there when we need it. The owner has no intention of using it until next spring."

"What were you checking out?"

It was an untactful question, interfering in a problem that was Frey's and only his.

Klammer realized immediately that he had gone too far.

"Forgive me." He was quick to reassure the Swede and make it clear he regretted putting a question he could see had irritated Frey. "Your preparations obviously have nothing to do with me. I have no doubt whatever steps you take will be appropriate and necessary."

"That's okay. There were two reasons why I went to the garage. The first was that I wanted to see how many people there were around in the morning. It's deserted shortly before nine. The only person I saw was an immigrant woman on her way to the laundry with an enormous pile of dirty washing and half a dozen snotty-nosed kids."

Klammer nodded with a smile. He was waiting for the rest of the story.

"I also wanted to establish what kind of license plate the car had."

"I'm with you. How long do you need to take over the car?"

"Three minutes at most. The plates will take the longest."

"Excellent."

Klammer looked pleased and smiled at Frey as if to show he was more than satisfied with the explanation. The Swede smiled back, but for quite different reasons. He was convinced his made-up story had been accepted. Lies, just like truth, only become plausible when they have been sprinkled with some simple, everyday images. The listener or reader has to be given some easily recognizable and credible picture he can take in before he starts getting suspicious. Every storyteller is aware of that, irrespective of whether he is a notorious yarn-spinner or a genuine truth-seeker.

"What happens in the morning is irrelevant," said Klammer. "We shan't need the car until about six in the evening. For two hours at most. I take it you agree the car should not be stolen at the last minute."

"Of course."

Klammer grinned wryly. It looked almost like an apology.

"You have been most cooperative, Mr. Frey. Not least because you haven't asked any questions. You must obviously have been wondering more than once just what my mission could be, not least because you have been involved without knowing quite what you're supposed to do, or what the target looks like. My silence must have been inconvenient for you. You must believe me when I tell you I would much rather have been frank with you. But I am bound by my orders, and I don't like them."

As soon as the German wanted to say something significant, he had an irritating habit of sounding like a bureaucrat. He had risen to his feet and was standing straight as a rod by the table. He suddenly stretched out his hand, quite unexpectedly, and Frey had no choice but to push back his chair and stand up as well. The handshake was forceful and manly. Possibly a little too insistent as far as the German was concerned. Frey could not help but notice, in passing, that Klammer was sweating profusely.

141

"We shan't see much of each other during the next few days," said Klammer, sounding more relaxed now. "My preparations will take up most of my time. If you find I don't avail myself of your kind hospitality one of these nights, you must not assume I have disappeared."

Once again, his face was dominated by his meager smile.

"Let's agree that we'll meet again here on Friday, at eleven o'clock."

"I'm with you," said Frey. "I'll be here."

A quarter of an hour later, shortly before ten in the morning, Klammer left the apartment. Frey wondered which of the exits he would use. The one through the grocer's premises was out of the question, business was in full swing.

It is true that lowering the venetian blinds on a chilly winter's day might appear rather strange, but Frey had not been able to think of any better way of letting Gudrun Brunhildson know Klammer was going out. Most probably he would take the underground. A glance at the timetable showed the next train was due in seven minutes. It sometimes happens that trains arrive late in the Stockholm underground, but they never leave a station before the scheduled time. Gudrun Brunhildson would have to stand out in the cold for a few minutes more before going through the barriers.

All in all, Frey was pleased with the way the morning had gone. The help he was getting from Gudrun Brunhildson was—as she had indicated—of enormous importance, and perhaps even crucial, despite the fact he was not yet sure why. Furthermore, his conversation with Klammer had provided him with a lot of useful information. The German was working together with somebody who could well be the one directing the whole operation. The time set for the liquidation, which is a more acceptable term for murder, was evidently something they could decide for themselves. There was a plan, and the victim was obviously a pawn in the game. Frey was not surprised, but he should have realized long ago

142

that Klammer had merely been ascribed a role, like himself: the role of executioner. As usual, the director was watching from a distance, without taking any risks.

Another piece of information, not insignificant, was that Klammer was starting to get nervous. His hands were still steady, but his wry smile was cropping up rather too often, and his palms had started to be sweaty.

ᐁ13

The full details of how Gudrun Brunhildson spent the next three days will never be known. It was a bitterly cold February day when she left Frey, and they would only meet on two more occasions before the dramatic event Klammer was planning as a climax to his stay in Stockholm.

One of the reasons, of course, is that Frey was the only one who knew what she was about. She reported to him. As far as everyone else was concerned, she was invisible, or just a shadow flitting by, a slight movement in the corner of one's eye, or an unconfirmed feeling of being watched.

When it was all over, Frey would display a tendency to dramatize and perhaps even overestimate her activities. When he met the Colonel in Berlin several months later, he described her efforts in such enthusiastic tones that the Colonel immediately suspected the exaggeration was due to Frey's appetite for chilled vodka, or possibly he had simply fallen in love with the woman who might be small but was nevertheless far from insignificant—not even in the Colonel's eyes.

Another and more intricate reason is that despite his long and intimate relationship with Gudrun Brunhildson, Frey had only a vague idea of the seriousness and determination with which she went about her business.

There is a widespread misunderstanding which proclaims that mutual confidence between two people must always be based on absolute honesty and scrupulous pursuit of the truth. This idea contains within it the seeds of a relationship's decline and, eventually, its acrimonious collapse. What seemed to be fellowship turns out to be subjection. What binds two people together in the long run is not truth or honesty, nor is it their love or their genuine efforts to meet each other halfway. The original burning desire to achieve a common goal very soon cools and is replaced by the hope of finding and keeping mutual interests at least. In the end, all that is left is the struggle that seemed self-evident at the beginning but later becomes a goal in itself: keeping going. By then, the collapse has become obvious to everybody. Paradoxically, what a relationship ought to be based on is in fact prospects rather than certainty of one's partner's loyalty and intentions. What leads to the final split is not only being caught in a lie.

Frey imagined Gudrun was his invisible eye, and as far as he was concerned, that was more than just a play on words. He admired her and trusted her. Sometimes he thought he was in love with her. Nevertheless, he never hesitated to make use of her services, which always meant he was exposing her to danger. In fact, he had belittled her and turned her into one of his tools. Needless to day, he would have rejected indignantly any such suggestion; Gudrun, however, was aware that their relationship was based on dependence. That was the difference between them. She realized it was necessary to create a balance in their relationship, and hence the pendulum swung over in her direction. Without his being aware of it, it was often she who steered his thoughts and laid the foundations of the decisions he made.

In many respects, Gudrun Brunhildson was just as taciturn as Jonas Mikael Frey. She was just as devious as he was when it came to role playing. Her honesty with him was never total, since she never attempted to adapt herself to him. She rarely lied to him, but there again, she did not tell him everything either. She had never told him, for instance, nor had she even hinted that she had a sparse but nevertheless extremely effective network of occasional assistants. They were people she could count on for help at any time. They were all from the same class: her own lower class. One was a waitress, another a porter, a third a taxi driver, a fourth a simple officeworker whose main task was to look after the mail, a fifth was probably an immigrant who earned enough money to pay his exorbitant rent in the Rinkeby ghetto by spending most of his waking life in a stark ticket booth at an underground station, and hence was in need of a little excitement and a bit of extra pocket money. Most of them owned her small favors of one kind or another, and paid her back by carrying out some of the simple tasks she set them.

They never asked her why she needed their help—that would have been impertinent. People who spend their lives in the basement of society always have deep respect for the integrity of their fellows. Most of what happens in this world is nobody else's business. Police and other authorities come up against stony silence. The press, radio, TV, social workers, and social researchers get the answers they want to hear, but they never get the truth. Silence and compliance are the only protection the underdog has against authority. Compliance does not necessarily mean subservience, and silence can often be turned into a weapon.

Jonas Frey was classless. That meant he could move fairly uninhibitedly in all levels of society. His work as a free-lance journalist opened many doors for him. He was very skillful in the art of bluff and at fitting into his environment. As a result, he was generally accepted if not liked more or less everywhere he went.

Although he disliked the intelligentsia, he liked to take part in their ego-tripping performances. He was just as likely to be found at a lively publishers' party among the self-proclaimed intellectuals as among insipid academics in some debating club or other where their overestimation of their own abilities took the form of insufferable volubility. He was sometimes employed by some advertising or public relations agency, where he would meet businessmen to whom it had never occurred that he might not be one of their own kind, albeit on a lower level. He sometimes mixed with politicians and higher civil servants, and they always treated him as a near-equal, although in fact they were not really sure who he was.

There were those who mistrusted him, some who feared him, and quite a lot more who avoided him. None of his acquaintances considered themselves to be particularly close to him, and few had any desire to be close. He had never pretended to be the sociable type.

The exceptions were the people he had links with for intelligence purposes. He had chosen them with the greatest of care, and none of them had any fear of his betraying them. On the contrary, in their eyes he was the solid rock in the new and secret world into which he had enticed them. They knew they would never be able to break free of him. There were times when they regretted what they had done, but regret does not do much good. It always comes too late. Hence he did all he could to ensure that the bonds he had ensnared them with remained invisible. Only very occasionally had he been forced to tighten the snare.

Frey never failed once he had decided to recruit someone new as a secret agent. He could not afford to fail—that would be the end of him. As a result, all the preparations he made before approaching someone for this purpose were elaborate and very carefully planned. They could take years sometimes. By the time he struck, he had all the cards in his hand.

It was like catching a fly in a dish of honey, and then hastening to rescue it from drowning.

His latest victim had been a stroke of luck. It was a disillusioned engineer who had been passed over; urged along by Frey, he had managed to transform his bitterness into a delightful feeling of being able to get his own back at last. The company the engineer worked for was in the process of developing a telecommunications system that would change the world, and although his access to secret material was limited, it was still considerable. He knew the company was on the way to becoming even richer and more powerful, thanks in no small measure to his own efforts; but even so, he could not count on much in the way of a pay raise. Others had already stolen his self-respect, so it was not very important anymore. For some time now he had been receiving sizable sums of money from Frey, and as far as he was concerned, the lack of public recognition was now fully compensated for by the feeling of malice mixed with the deep satisfaction he derived from knowing he had avenged himself. Injustice can only be made good by one's own infamy, and the feeling of pleasure it brings is not lessened by the fact that one is not found out.

Klammer had started acting like a professional. He kept an eye on the elevator leading down to the underground platform, and was the last to get on the train as the doors closed. There were not many passengers at this time of day. The biggest group was a horde of screaming kindergarten children and their teachers heading for the Skansen open-air museum. Several of the children were thrilled to find a new lady to play with, especially as she was of a size that suited them much more than their real teachers. One of the little girls clung on to her coat and refused to let go. To her great disappointment, her new friend got out at the very next station; the girl would have been most upset if she knew the little lady was simply changing cars.

148

It was cold out. The thermometer reading was more than twenty below, but the sun was shining down from a frosty blue sky and the three crowns on the tower of the City Hall glittered like jewels and were reflected in the ice on Riddarfjärden Bay. Despite the cold, most of the pedestrians felt there was a touch of spring in the air. They could sense it in the way the snow crystals were shining on the railings separating the railway from the pedestrian walkway on Central Bridge, between Tegelbacken and Riddarholmen Island. There were at least ten people between Klammer and Gudrun Brunhildson, and although the German was in no great hurry and even took time to enjoy the view of Scandinavia's most beautiful city, she had no fear of being discovered.

It was only when, instead of continuing toward the Old Town, Klammer turned in the direction of Riddarholms Church and then took the next street on the right that Gudrun hesitated, wondering how best to continue tailing him. She could see the German's back between the cars parked outside the Svea Hovrätt Law Courts. Behind the closed doors of the austere, unwelcoming facade, blind but not always impartial justice held sway, and there was nowhere she could conceal herself. The cobbled streets around here were very slippery, and there was not a soul to be seen. Klammer continued his walk up the hill toward the Kammarkollegiet building, and when he turned around at the brow, he was pleased to see he was alone.

Klammer could hardly leave Riddarholmen without Gudrun knowing—there is just one bridge linking the island with the Old Town, apart from the narrow footbridge leading to Tegelbacken. It can sometimes be advisable not to overdo things when shadowing someone. One can never overlook the fact that some people have highly developed intuition and can feel when they are being watched. In such cases, it is important to give them opportunities to check whether they are being followed; after several negative checks, caution can sometimes be replaced by an easygoing sense of security. Klammer had made at least four such checks on his way to Riddarholmen, and Gudrun was not surprised when she saw him again at the brow of the hill. The square at the bottom and the street leading up from it were both as empty as they had been before, and when he turned to continue on his way, she could tell from his walk that he had now made up his mind: There was no one behind him. He was starting to feel secure.

Gudrun was not impressed by his choice of a meeting place—there was no longer any doubt about it: Klammer had arranged to meet someone here on the island. It is true that there was not much chance of happening on an acquaintance or a busybody on the deserted, wintry shores of the island, but there again, whoever had chosen this isolated spot was making the meeting unnecessarily prominent.

It is easier to remain unnoticed in a crowd of people. Gudrun would have preferred one of the market halls or one of the self-service restaurants, which would inevitably be crowded at lunchtime here in the city center, where office-workers exchange luncheon vouchers for standardized food.

A thoughtful and slightly sarcastic smile spread over Gudrun's face. She had difficulty in shaking off a suspicion that in fact did not amuse her in the least. She had begun to recognize the behavior pattern and thought she knew its origin. The suspicion must be checked out. Without hesitation, she started to follow the same route taken by Klammer a few minutes earlier; there was virtually no risk of him coming back the same way.

The person Klammer had arranged to meet must have been waiting on the quayside, since he was with the German when Gudrun saw them, strolling slowly along the quay. Even from this distance, she could see that the other man was doing most of the talking. It looked almost as if Klammer was being given orders. When the two men stopped at the point where the nostalgic Göta Canal boats generally moor in summer, though now the ice was piled up in contorted chunks, he was standing more or less at attention, as if talking to a superior. Neither of them seemed to be the least bit interested in the incredible view of bluish-tinted, ice-covered Riddarfjärden Bay. Far away in the distance was the outline of the mighty Västerbron Bridge, and beyond that you could just make out Askrikefjärden Bay and the snow-laden parks and woods of Drottningholm.

Klammer was talking to a Russian. Gudrun had been right. The preference Russians have for meeting in out-of-the-way places is a standing joke among their opponents. If possible, they would really prefer to meet on a desert island, and everyone involved should preferably make their way there in their own rowboat—or so the Americans and British claim. That may be, but there again, there is no denying that the CIA or MI5 rarely know where the island is situated, or when the boat trip will take place.

Gudrun recognized the Russian immediately. Although they were over eighty yards away and she had the dazzling sun in her eyes as she peered through the railings in a fence, she could see without any shadow of doubt that Herwart Klammer had traveled from Sundbyberg to Riddarholmen in order to meet the technical attaché of the Russian trade delegation in Stockholm, Dr. Dimitri Gusov.

There was no need for Gudrun to stay at her lookout post any longer. She had seen enough. There was no sign of anything to worry about, and she was quite sure no other discreet persons were displaying any interest in the conversation between the Russian and the East German. After all, if there had not been two remarkable circumstances, the meeting could not have been described as startling. There were no doubt several thousand people from Eastern bloc in Stockholm, and that two of them should have chosen to go for a walk in the wintry sunshine along Riddarholmen quay is no more remarkable than a Swede and an American meeting in Red Square in Moscow, or perhaps preferably the more attractive Alexandrovski Gardens nearby. However, they would both no doubt be able to produce some kind of current identity papers if anyone from the KGB had become curious.

Herwart Klammer had no current identity papers. He was in Stockholm illegally, and had borrowed his identity from a fellow-countryman who had spent most of his time in more or less voluntary house arrest at the East German embassy. When that Herwart Klammer left Sweden and returned home, he resumed his own name but left behind his doppelgänger. This fact alone ought to have worried the Swedish security forces. If on top of that they had been aware that not only was the German's presence known to the Russians but that there was also good reason to suppose Klammer was in their pay, it is likely the affair would have been given top priority and SÄPO would have been placed on red alert.

When Gudrun drew back from her vantage point, she felt pleased and satisfied. The discovery that Klammer was in league with the Russians must mean that Frey had finally obtained one of the missing pieces of his jigsaw puzzle. The picture was beginning to take shape.

It was not until a quarter of an hour later that she started to feel uneasy.

Directly opposite the Riddarhuset building on the Riddarholmen side, there is a spot where you can see both the Central Bridge and the Riddarholms Bridge, and that is where Gudrun was stationed. There was not much in the way of cover, but she had no choice.

Gusov and Klammer ought to have split up some time ago—intimate meetings of this nature are always quick and businesslike. There is no time for a trivial chat. Gudrun assumed they would not appear together, and it seemed natural for the German to come first: A subaltern always takes leave of his superior and is sent packing with due ceremony, never the reverse. That was why she was both confused and surprised when she saw the Russian marching briskly along, seemingly unconcerned. There was no sign of Klammer anywhere.

There are times when one has to choose between waiting to see what happens next and changing one's plans altogether. In such circumstances, there is sometimes no time for a thorough analysis of the alternatives. It is natural, therefore, to hesitate, but that cannot go on for long. One must not hold back for fear of following up a new idea or a new lead—the suspicion one might be missing an opportunity is in conflict with the built-in reluctance to deviate from a well-thought-out and hitherto successful plan. In the end, the choice is a question of temperament, experience, and self-confidence. The judgment comes a long time after, as do the excuses, should they be needed.

Gudrun Brunhildson was used to coping with unexpected situations. She was flexible and independent. Even so, she hesitated; but not for long. When Gusov stopped for the red light at the Munkbroleden crossing, she made up her mind. The German would have to wait, for the time being at least. Something inside her convinced her that just at the moment, Dr. Gusov was the more interesting of the two.

As she walked toward Mälartorget Square, she became increasingly convinced she had done the right thing. She was not in the least put out when she thought she caught a glimpse of Klammer on the other side of the railway lines— she recognized the peculiar narrow-brimmed hat he insisted on wearing, irrespective of the way it looked on him. Gudrun had overlooked the pedestrian walkway over the Hebbe railway bridge. Klammer certainly knew the quickest and least obtrusive way to get from Riddarholmen to the Old Town underground station, and she had to admire he was thorough and had planned things in meticulous detail; his knowledge of the Stockholm public transport system was most impressive. She had to admit he had behaved in a professional way; the question was had she? Despite everything, she felt a little bit uncomfortable when she could no longer see his narrow-brimmed hat bobbing along. It seemed as if she had committed a sin of omission when she decided to stop following him.

It's no use crying over spilled milk, and so she gritted her teeth and concentrated on the Russian some eighty yards ahead of her, striding purposefully toward Mälartorget. The problem of catching up with Klammer again could wait until later. Deep down, Gudrun Brunhildson was a fatalist. Moreover, she had to reconcile herself to the fact that she could not be in more than one place at a time.

"There were two taxis waiting at the station," said Gudrun. "You get lucky sometimes. He took one of them, and I just managed to get the other at the last minute."

"You went direct to the exhibition center?" asked Frey.

"Yes."

"He didn't seem worried about being followed?"

"Not in the least. When I realized where he was heading, I gave him a few minutes start. We were overtaken by a third taxi just before the entrance to the center. I recognized her straightaway. It was Gerd Angerbo. When we pulled up outside the main entrance, she'd just paid off the driver and was rushing up the steps in the direction of her office. She looked nervous."

"No one noticed you, I hope."

Gudrun chuckled.

"Of course not. Gerd Angerbo was far too scared to notice anybody as insignificant as I am. You know how it is. Nobody sees people like me. Not in daylight at least. It's only at night that anybody recognizes a waitress—assuming, of course, she is still playing the part of a waitress. The same applies to a cashier at a supermarket. When she's off work, she belongs to the lower classes, and obviously, nobody would ever dream of mixing with the likes of her."

Frey nodded in agreement.

"You're quite sure it was Gerd Angerbo the Russian had gone to meet?"

"When I got to reception they were both on their way into her office. I watched them closing the door behind them. The girl at the switchboard recognized me though. She acknowledged me, 'cause we're two of a kind. The rest put me out of their minds the moment they saw me."

"Didn't she wonder why you were there?"

"Who?"

"The telephonist."

"Why should she? There's a nonstop stream of visitors passing through those corridors, even when there isn't an exhibition on. Lots of them are applying for jobs in the restaurant. She knows I'm a free lance, and nobody is surprised to bump into one of those. You ought to know that."

"And then?"

"I found the restaurant manager and spoke to him for a few minutes. If I like, I can have a job there in a couple of weeks. Then I went out to the courtyard again and waited. The Russian appeared five minutes later and took the first taxi—presumably it was the one I'd ordered. The next one took so long that I knew I'd lost him. Just then Gerd Angerbo came rushing out through the door and took it for granted the waiting taxi was hers. But I had a piece of luck for the second time today: a third cab turned up quickly enough for me to be able to follow Gerd."

"Good," said Frey. "Where was she off to?"

As she did not reply immediately, he turned around for the first time and looked at her in profile.

"Where was she off to?"

"She headed into Östermalm and got out at the entrance of an apartment block in Kommendörsgatan," replied Gudrun, and there was a note of triumph in her voice.

"I thought she lived in Solna."

"Oh, so you know that."

155

There was a touch of irony in her voice, and Frey wondered to himself just how much she knew that he had never suspected.

"She mentioned it sometime or other," he said lamely.

"Anyway, I managed to get into the entrance hall and read the nameplates."

"Anything interesting?"

"I should say so. One of the tenants is Alf Skolle."

"The press secretary?"

"Who else could it be?"

She heard Frey catch his breath, and without looking at him, she knew he was biting his lower lip.

"I won't pretend I'm surprised, but I can understand if you're confused."

"You didn't follow her upstairs, I suppose?"

"No. What good would that have done?"

He felt he had been put in his place, and neither of them said a word.

They were sitting a few yards apart on one of the benches at the Huvudsta underground station. So far they were alone, apart from an elderly couple who had missed the previous train. Now things were starting to happen again, and a few new passengers were on their way down the escalator to the platform. None of the new arrivals would ever have guessed the two of them sitting on the bench were acquainted with each other. They were staring straight ahead as they talked, and it was only when you were close up that you could see their lips moving.

"You've done well," said Frey. "Extremely well. As usual."

"I've had a bit of luck above all else," said Gudrun.

They could hear the rails beginning to hum and knew a train was coming. Frey turned toward Gudrun once more.

"What are you thinking of doing now?" he asked.

"Looking for Herwart Klammer. Or have you any other suggestions?"

She smiled at him, and he thought she looked so incredibly full of life. Then she stood up and got into the nearest car.

As the train started moving in the direction of Stockholm, Frey was still sitting on the bench. He looked solemn, thoughtful; as if he had difficult problems to wrestle with. It is not unusual on the Stockholm underground to see a man or a woman lost in thought. Nobody could care less, as they say nowadays. It is rare for anyone to try and share somebody else's problems, or give them active help in solving them. Gudrun was determined to give Frey all the help she could. She would find Klammer, and try to find out if he had arranged to meet anyone else. The only snag was, she was not at all clear how to go about finding him.

14

The rest of the day turned out quite differently from what Gerd Angerbo had imagined, or feared. This was due partly to the fact that she did not have all her emotions under control when she got out of the taxi at Skolle's apartment. She raced up the stairs as if she were only too keen to act on a decision whose consequences she could not possibly have worked out properly as yet.

The cab ride had given her an opportunity of pulling herself together after the conversation with Dr. Gusov, but not completely. She was eager to go and impatient, and during the last hour she had changed emotions as often as a chameleon changes color.

For the first few minutes her thoughts were in a state of absolute chaos. When she tumbled into the taxi out at the exhibition center she was excited and on edge. Gusov's generous but crafty offer had thrown her into confusion. She had appreciated the hidden threat behind what he had said, but she had not been able to analyze the situation in peace and quiet. Calm, meditative thought was an occupation Gerd Angerbo seldom indulged in. As far as she was concerned, action was the thing, and with a certain amount of justification, she considered herself to have feelers sufficiently sensitive to save her in most situations.

The most natural reaction for anyone under a threat is to try and run away from it. Women have always started running in order to shake off real or imagined pursuers, especially when they're alone, and above all at night when there are not many people about and every man in a doorway could be dangerous. Only when the outside door back home shuts behind them, and the lock falls into place with that definitive, confidence-inspiring click, can they breathe freely again, and sometimes even giggle to themselves. Fear is not always logical, and for a short while it can make the victim blind. One's heart very quickly resumes its normal speed in the protected environment of one's own home, and the adrenaline begins to ebb. Excitement and fear are replaced by a feeling of emptiness. Even so, one does not always feel right. Relief that it is all over is sometimes tinged with a stale feeling of shame.

Gerd Angerbo was a woman, and she fled; but like all hunted game, she slowed down after a while, thinking she was out of range of her pursuer.

At Hornstull the traffic started to build up and her taxi was forced to stop at one of the red lights. In the car that pulled up alongside Gerd, barely an arm's length away, was a charming, well-dressed man of just the right age. He indicated clearly his appreciation of her, and waved as if inviting her to get to know him better, or regretting the fact that they would never see each other again. Gerd could not help giving him one of her very best smiles in response. The brief moment of intimacy, the unfulfilled meeting hampered by the frosty windowpanes and growing increasingly blurred before fading away in the poisonous yellow fumes from the car exhausts, was sufficient to give her the strength to cast aside her uneasiness. Being admired from a distance, the merest hint of a possibility, can brighten up a whole day and drive away the gloomiest of apprehensions.

The danger was over for the time being. At least she felt it was. How could a woman find better protection from an unpleasant man than by finding another, well-disposed man? The knowledge that the world was full of men, and knowing what to do in order to get them on her side, filled her with confidence. She had no possibility of breaking free from Dimitri Gusov just at the moment, but from now on, the game would continue on equal terms. Now was the time to show what female cunning and artfulness could do.

The money would be a great help. It was not until they were passing Slussen that it really dawned on her how big a sum it really was. She would have to reckon with a few reductions. Mind you, she could not see any reason why Alf Skolle should get more than a small amount. A bit more than usual, perhaps, but no more than fifteen thousand kronor at any rate. That should be enough. Alf Skolle would steal anything for fifteen thousand kronor. Larceny was all he was capable of.

She wanted to get out of Sweden, and she would need help to flee. With a nod of affirmation, Gerd made one vital decision. She would confess everything to Jonas Mikael Frey, holding nothing back. That would mean the end of their cooperation. She could imagine his reaction, his restrained anger, and his consternation. She had been playing a double game, and the trust between them would be gone forever. Nevertheless, she knew he would not let her down. He had no choice, in fact. Given the circumstances, it would be a relief for him as well if she left the country.

Gerd was conscious of the fact that she was an important link in Frey's chain of communication, possibly even the most important, but not the only one. Now she had transformed herself into a threat, not only to Frey, but to all the rest of his network, and threats have to be eliminated. There is only one effective way of getting rid of a threat, and she knew what that was. Hence, she must obtain guarantees to secure her own life and her own future.

She spent a little while wondering how much money she ought to offer Frey. She had always found it difficult to give away anything that belonged to her, and always looked for alternative solutions. She suddenly realized she had capital that would be of value to him, but would be worthless to her the moment she left Sweden. She made up her mind on the spot. Although she had sworn never to reveal her contacts to anybody, she was now prepared to hand them over to Frey, without their permission, and without even asking them.

A few names and addresses on a piece of paper was all that was needed. All things considered, it would be a mistake to try and bribe Frey, with money, at least. He was one of those very few people who are not for sale. Gerd wrinkled her nose. The thought frightened her, but that did not mean he rose in her estimation on that account.

She would take out all the money she had in the bank and put it into dollars. Gerd knew to the last öre how much she had. When she emigrated to the United States she would arrive as a wealthy professional Swedish woman in midcareer. The Americans would not hesitate to let her in. There was not a single blot in her papers that might make them suspicious; on the contrary, she was the kind of person they are always ready to welcome with open arms.

There could not be any connection between Gusov and Frey, she was quite sure of that. Frey had always warned her against responding to any approaches from the Russians. He had even spread the word that she was working for SÄPO.

Frey had concentrated on gathering technical information, she was certain. The step to the much more sensitive and more dangerous military and political espionage is a big one, even in the various spheres sometimes overlap. Industrial espionage is more wide-ranging and more difficult to survey, and there are a lot of one-shot deals between people working with drawings, computers, and electronics. That makes the risk of exposure much smaller. It is true that industry has started to use its own security services, but they are generally understaffed, and although they are a good financial investment, they are cut back ruthlessly whenever budgets are trimmed.

Gerd was aware of all this. She also knew how difficult it was to find suitable people in the key positions needed to coordinate and lead the gathering of information. This was one of the reasons why she was convinced Frey and his employers would be pleased to see her transplanted to America. It was likely they would help her to establish herself in her new country. She would get a new contact person, someone like Frey in many respects, although he would never put as much faith in her loyalty. Just as discreetly, this American would support her efforts to find a job corresponding to her qualifications, and one that would be a useful source of information in the future. Once she started climbing up the ladder and began to establish herself, they would leave her in peace. With luck, they'd leave her on her own for five years. A newly planted agent is a tender plant that must not be exposed to drafts, not even when it has taken root. Only when it has burst into full bloom can one be certain it will bear fruit.

It was a determined Gerd Angerbo who stepped out of the taxi outside Skolle's front door. She felt she had recovered completely from her conversation with Dr. Gusov and was ready to take on the unreliable press secretary.

Perhaps she had already started to get overconfident, as she omitted to check whether she was being followed. On the other hand, it is doubtful she would have paid much attention to the taxi that turned into the street shortly after her own. Just for a moment, it seemed to be slowing down, but immediately afterward it picked up speed and continued to the next crossroads. It is also unlikely Gerd would have recognized the short lady in the backseat of the cab even if she had caught a glimpse of her. Her appearance had changed altogether, and she looked nothing like the frightened little thing Gerd had stormed past on the steps leading up to the exhibition center office.

A bottle of German wine sat in a cooler on the table. Alf Skolle had been out shopping. He was still at an age when a reasonably healthy man can recover from a rough patch surprisingly quickly, irrespective of whether the wounds were self-inflicted or not. He looked devastated, it is true, and his skin was blotchy and unhealthy, but he had regained that self-confident look in his cornflower-blue eyes, and there was quite a bit of cockiness in him when he thrust out his arms to embrace her.

"Behold a man risen from the dead," he announced, grinning broadly. "Did the manager invite you to lunch?"

"No," replied Gerd with a smile. "We're not on those terms, I'm afraid."

"Mean bastard."

She made it clear how pleased she was to see that Skolle had got a grip on himself. The apartment was still untidy, but he had made an effort to clear away the worst of it. He had taken a shower, and his breath was no longer foul. The hand holding the cigarette was almost steady. Only the twitching of his eyelids betrayed the fact that he was not yet quite restored.

He had recovered his powers of observation, and noticed immediately that she was bursting, as if she found it difficult to hold back what she was dying to say. They were sitting on opposite sides of the table, the unopened bottle of wine between them. He reached out toward the cooler, then had second thoughts.

"Let's hear it, then," he said, and there was a chill in his voice already.

"I only exchanged a few words with the exhibition manager," said Gerd cautiously. "Actually, it wasn't only for his sake I was called to the exhibition center."

163

"Really . . . ?"

Skolle's smile froze on his lips and was exchanged by a sly and suspicious expression. It was always the same with her. She never came to see him without an ulterior motive. A few hours ago he had been dreaming about their spending a few days together with no obligations, no business obligations and counterobligations. Just two grown-up people who enjoyed being together. He ought to have known it was only a dream.

"You met . . . him?"

Gerd nodded.

Skolle sighed, and his face clouded over.

"What did he want this time?"

"To begin with, he wanted you back at work by tomorrow morning."

"I'm off sick."

"Not any more you aren't."

Skolle turned sour. Wasn't shattering his dreams enough? Now she was ordering him about as well. He had never been able to stand being talked to like that.

"Who does he think he is?" She did not answer. "Does he think I'm some kind of puppet he can manipulate whenever he feels like it?"

"No," answered Gerd. "You're no marionette. In his eyes—and in mine, too—you are a very important man. But every so often opportunities arise that can't be forseen, but which must not be missed."

"What do you mean?"

"Unless you think your sick leave is worth more money than twenty-five thousand kronor, he wants you to do him a favor. Maybe one last favor."

She regretted those words as soon as she had said them. Sometimes she acted far too impetuously. In fact, she had no hope of holding herself in check. She noticed how he had changed completely in the space of only a few seconds, and for a moment, she was afraid he might lapse into a sort of

164

childish obstinacy. She had seen him like that before. It could take her hours, even days, to talk him around. That was why she had offered him ten thousand kronor more than she had intended from the start. She could forget about the money; much more serious was the fact that she had hinted their cooperation might be nearing its end.

"What was that you said?"

"Twenty-five thousand kronor," she answered quickly, but this time the rapid reply was completely intentional. "You heard me right."

She waited, and to her relief Skolle soon started to chuckle. He licked his lips, and if it had not been for the slight twitching of his eyelids, he would have managed to look like a mischievous little schoolboy.

The cunning glint reappeared in his eyes, which seemed to shrink. He looked not unlike a pimp who has begun to suspect the percentage he is getting from one of his girls does not quite tally.

"Did you say twenty-five thousand?" he asked. "Are you sure he didn't mean thirty-five?"

She shook her head angrily, as if any such thought were offensive. Even so, he did not seem to be convinced she was telling the truth.

"It's about time he started to appreciate my full value," he said loftily. "He should have done that a long time ago. No doubt you're also getting a cut?"

"Of course."

"How much?"

"Half of what you're getting," she lied, and almost spat out the words. "I have no secrets from you, and the very thought that I would . . ."

"It's not that, he interrupted. "But in future I'll deal with him myself—at least as far as financial arrangements are concerned."

"That's out of the question."

The reply shot out like a rifle bullet, and Skolle shied

165

back. His cockiness was superficial, and Gerd could see it flaking off in large lumps. She had to try hard to conceal her contempt, and instead, smiled while waiting for him to regain his composure. There was something doglike in his expression when their eyes met again.

"It's just that you have to be protected," said Gerd solicitously.

"I understand that."

"You're much too valuable to us," she went on. "We can't allow ourselves to take any unnecessary risks. The present arrangement is for the good of us all from the security point of view."

Skolle said nothing.

"I'll tell him what you said." Gerd looked entreatingly at him. "I'm quite sure what he'll say, though."

They sat in silence for a while. Skolle was tapping away absentmindedly on the wine bottle, which was still unopened on the table in front of them. He did not seem completely satisfied, yet neither was he obstinate. There was still something bothering him, and the cunning glint kept appearing in his eyes. She knew he was unpredictable, pusillanimous, and false, but she had also learned not to underestimate him. He could be prompted and pushed to a certain point, but she would never be able to rely on him. His weakest point was his vanity.

"One last favor, did you say?"

Her eyes flashed. He had memorized every word she had said.

"I didn't mean it quite like that," she said softly, trying to sound casual. "He just indicated we ought to lie low for a while after this business."

"Business?"

"You are being pedantic with words," she said with a laugh. "Twenty-five thousand is not bad business, wouldn't you say? For just one little favor that'll take only a few hours to carry out."

Twenty-five thousand kronor.

Money has an amazing way of affecting how people think and act. Alf Skolle was practically broke. After that day's shopping, he had just one hundred-kronor note left in his wallet, and it would be another two weeks before he was paid again. He had overdrawn his checking account and used his credit card to the limit of what was legally permitted. A few hours earlier he had decided to ask Gerd for a loan, knowing she would not refuse.

"When do we get paid?"

It was a crude and specific question, but in fact logical and even crucial for anyone short of cash. Long-term implications usually shrink and difficult decisions become easier to make when they are associated with an acute shortage of money.

Gerd gave him an understanding smile. It was not the first time Skolle had been without money. The prospects of a little advance would make it easier for him to make up his mind. She would not even need to wave money under his nose to ensure he would be back at his desk the next morning. The only lingering doubt she had was whether to lend him two thousand kronor, or just one.

"Probably on Monday," she answered with a smile.

Skolle drew himself up and suddenly looked manly again. With an exaggeratedly elegant flourish, he lifted the bottle out of the cooler, opened it with a loud pop, poured out a glass for each of them, and raised his glass in a toast.

"I'll do it," he said solemnly. "On condition I don't have to use force."

"No, no," she assured him quickly. "Of course not."

It had been much easier than she had thought. She had not even had to explain just what she wanted him to do.

There is a time for frivolity and a time for being serious. Suddenly, and in unison, both Gerd Angerbo and Alf Skolle were transformed into committee people. Somewhere deep

167

down they were both bureaucrats who knew how to carry out a delicate operation. They were meticulous in adhering to the prescribed rules.

They very soon discovered there were surprisingly few details that needed discussing, but this did not prevent them from going through them very carefully. Skolle had heard rumors about the memo concerning the border between Sweden and the Soviet Union in the Baltic—there were very few important matters in public administration that were not known about very soon, at least in outline, by far too many civil servants. He thought it probable he would see the memorandum—the minister generally consulted him whenever there was some delicate problem to make decisions about. On the other hand, it was doubtful whether he would be left alone with the secret documents at any time.

"Nevertheless," said Skolle, "I do have to read through the papers in peace and quiet if I'm going to be able to express an opinion, so it's not impossible."

"How long do you need?"

"A few minutes. The camera is very fast and reliable. The only problem would be if the documents contained maps on larger-sized paper than standard."

Chance, circumstances, coincidence would have to dictate what happened. Skolle was prepared to take the risk, but he did not intend to do anything to force the situation. Gerd agreed with his point of view. No matter what, their first priority must be to avoid exposure. Under no circumstances must they be caught. They judged the odds to be around fifty-fifty, but even so, Gerd had a strong feeling that Skolle would succeed. This was partly due to the fact that Dr. Gusov had thus far never miscalculated. Her intuition told her they would pull it off. She did not have much time for probability theory, but she did believe in luck, and luck must not desert her now, at the eleventh hour.

"There's just one thing I don't understand," said Skolle.

"How can he be so sure this memorandum will be sent to us tomorrow or the day after?"

"It'll come on Friday."

"How can he know that?"

"I asked him, and for once he answered," said Gerd. "I got the impression he has another source of information in important places. Someone who knows what is being prepared for the next cabinet meeting but who doesn't have direct access to the documents."

Skolle pondered.

"The Foreign Office," he said. "All ministries leak, but the FO leaks like a sieve. The Cabinet Office on the other hand is usually pretty secure. Even so, there's no end of rumors."

"Our friend is not satisfied with rumors. He wants black on white."

"A pedantic point of view," said Skolle, reaching for the bottle again.

It is natural for tension to ease after a decision has been made that both parties consider irrevocable. For a while, Gerd Angerbo and Alf Skolle were like two conspirators who have hit upon a course of mutual benefit. What they needed to do now was to prevent worries from creeping in, for no matter how much they laughed and joked and claimed for each other's benefit they were looking forward to the next couple of days with confidence, they still had a nagging residue of insecurity and fear deep down. The easiest way for Skolle to keep his spirits up was to drink a few more glasses of German wine. He tried to play the part of a carefree man, and as usual, his act was the key factor in bringing off his mission. He had no loyalty at all to anyone or anything other than himself. What other people regarded as theft or treachery, he calculated in terms of money. When he was on his own or together with Gerd Angerbo, he occasionally stepped out of character, but never at vital moments. He could drink himself legless and carry on like a pig, he could cry and act like a stubborn little child on a cot, but the moment he stepped on the stage, he was identical with whatever role he had taken upon himself. The stage, acting, playing parts—that was the only thing which kept him going. Nothing else mattered. He had discovered very early on that life has nothing of value to offer.

Gerd Angerbo was more restrained. She was taken up by the thought that here she was at last, on the brink of something vital and conclusive. She had won, and the dream of a new, different, and promising future filled her with happiness and pride. Alf Skolle meant nothing to her, not even her contempt for him. He had served his purpose, and she would be free of him the moment he dropped his camera into her handbag. She made no effort to suppress her worries. She knew she would be nervous when it came to the crunch, but she also knew she would not panic. It would all be over in less than five minutes. The risks were more serious this time, but no greater than they had been before. Even if she heard Alf Skolle had been caught, she would still have a realistic chance of getting away with it. Gusov had stressed that point in particular. If she understood him correctly, he was prepared to sacrifice Alf Skolle in order to save Gerd Angerbo. That was logical and quite understandable. Gusov could never be linked with Skolle, but on this occasion, too, he would actually come into physical contact with Gerd Angerbo.

15

Gudrun Brunhildson was not superstitious, but she did have premonitions. Perhaps that is why she went a little bit over the top in her conversation with Frey. She felt on edge, as if she were itching all over. She sometimes found it difficult to stop giggling. It was her way of bottling up her tension as the vital moment drew nearer and nearer.

"You must stay at home all day tomorrow," said Frey.

She did not answer, but nodded as if she were assenting. In practice, she had no intention of obeying the order.

"I'm out sick for the whole week," she said.

"Get yourself an alibi. Invite somebody over for coffee, or make sure somebody sees you in the laundry."

They had met on the platform of the Vreten underground station. Frey preferred to meet on underground stations. He generally chose one of the suburbs, where the trains emptied quickly and the inhospitable platforms were more or less deserted for long periods. Every new arrival at a place like this always had to start off by making the painfully slow journey down the escalator, wide open to prying eyes and easily identifiable all the way down. Having reached platform level, such people stand no chance of creeping within earshot and listening to a conversation without being noticed. There were just a few screaming schoolboys careering up and down in large groups; everybody else kept at a respectful distance from other passengers.

Gudrun had come to Vreten in order to submit her final report. She had been working for several weeks now, with just short breaks for sleep. It may well be she had shrunk even more, but her eyes were still wide awake, and there was no sign of exhaustion in her expression.

She had an admirable way of preserving her strength, and she knew how to make the most of every opportunity of productive rest. The journey time from T-Centralen to Vreten was only ten minutes, but she had slept for eight of them. When the train started to slow down as it approached the station, she woke up; it was as straightforward as having a reliable alarm clock built into her brain. The transformation from being asleep to being awake was as natural as catching up with her own shadow under a streetlight.

Frey had been in another car at the very front of the train, and when he saw Gudrun step out onto the platform last of all, he was struck by her energy and the alertness of her bearing.

"Alf Skolle turned up at the ministry this morning," she reported. "He seemed in control of himself, and he appeared to be in good health again."

"I don't quite see where he fits into the puzzle," said Frey.

"He's her lover."

"Okay. But might he not be a bit more than that?"

He looked displeased, as if the straightforward explanation had been too glib.

You think you've been let down, she thought. In more then one way, perhaps. You think you ought to know all about Gerd Angerbo, but now you know she's let you down.

172

You've never claimed she was one of yours, that's true. And so it should be. Even I would deny knowing you, except as a fleeting acquaintance, if anybody started asking questions.

"And the woman?"

He avoided mentioning Gerd by name in order to try and hint that she was not all that important. It was quite illogical, but aimed at blunting the sharp edge of Gudrun's unspoken accusation.

"Gerd Angerbo left Alf Skolle's apartment shortly after eleven o'clock. She had put her finery on and taken a taxi straight into town. I followed her in my own car and was forced to park on Hamngatan, which cost me a two-hundred-kronor fine."

"Where did she go?"

"To the bank. She had a long talk with the accountant in the foreign section, then she had to wait for nearly a quarter of an hour before she was called. She signed lots of papers, but she didn't make any withdrawals as far as I could see."

"She's getting ready to run for it," muttered Frey. "At the very least, she's going abroad."

He could have added that he was not surprised at this anymore. He was furious and also disappointed that Gerd had not informed him of her plans. There was no point. The only conclusion he could draw with any certainty was that he could no longer trust her.

"What happened next?"

"She went and had lunch. At the Riche. That lady is used to living in style."

"Was she on her own?"

"In a way. There was nobody else at her table. The first half hour or so nothing happened at all, and I was wondering whether I might as well go when four gentlemen turned up at the restaurant. One of them was Dimitri Gusov. Two of the others also looked like Russians, but the fourth was a Swede. He works at the Foreign Office."

"How do you know that?"

In point of fact, it was outrageous of him to query her information.

Gudrun gave him a scornful smile that he ought to have seen through if he had not been surly and irritated. For once she was prepared to reveal how she went about her business. If nothing else, it might at least put him in a better mood.

"Very simple," she said. "I asked."

Her ridiculously simple explanation surprised him, and he looked almost foolish.

"I couldn't ask the maître d', of course," she went on. "In any case, it's by no means sure he would have let me into the dining room—not just because he's a stuck-up jerk, but mainly because I've worked there once or twice. There's an unwritten rule in the restaurant trade that says staff mustn't mix with the guests. Not even when they're off duty, and in any case, not at a place where they work."

Frey muttered something. He was starting to get impatient.

"But there's always a way. I've known the old man who runs the cloakroom for ages. He's a bit of a dirty old man and easy to get talking. If you let him have a bit of a grope, he's got nothing against a little chat. Customers tend to come and go at about the same time, and a visit from somebody like me helps to pass the time in between."

Gudrun was grinning broadly. Frey was not one of those who approved of playing around, and she could see how he was puckering up his lips. What was he picturing to himself? A wrinkled old hand under her skirt stroking her thighs, and clawlike fingers squeezing her breasts? So what? Was that any worse to accept than a picture of someone with a bullet in her chest, choking on her own blood?

"The old man's an excellent source of information," she continued. "There isn't a man or woman of note he can't identify. Nowadays people even use a charge card to pay the cloakroom fee; so he gets to know not only who they are but

174

what they do. Plus, he often gets to know their weaknesses. A bar is an excellent place for finding out about people."

Frey nodded. He was still not amused.

"Right at the back, at the end of the hat rack, there's a spare stool he lets me sit on," said Gudrun, teasingly. "Even if I hoist my skirt up, nobody can see what's going on from the entrance hall. It's much too dark in there. In any case, customers at places like that never notice the staff, they're far too occupied with themselves."

She'd gone far enough.

"Did they talk to each other?" asked Frey. His voice was harsh. "The Russian and Gerd Angerbo?"

"Of course. Not for very long, and they wanted it to look as if they'd met by accident. You know how it is. Somebody comes out of the ladies and bumps into a man in the hallway quite by accident. It doesn't need to be somebody very familiar, it's the same if they barely know each other. Needless to say, a woman of the world has to say hello and show him how delighted she is to see him. You never know, somebody else might be watching, somebody she knows. It's what's called being among the in crowd nowadays."

For the first time, Frey smiled. It looked as if she had succeeded in putting him back in a good mood.

"You're surely not going to tell me Gerd Angerbo hugged the Russian and gave him a kiss?" he said with a grin.

"Not far off. It's a sort of conditioned reflex among posh ladies nowadays, which is supposed to give them a touch of Frenchness. I don't quite see how it fits in with modern ideas on gender roles. Most Swedish men I know seem put out by it. Still, she managed to stop herself in time. Gusov certainly isn't the kind of person you'd want to hug."

"Nor have any other sort of contact with."

"He'd been waiting for her," said Gudrun quietly. "No question about it. His interest in the display cases with expensive crystal vases in the vestibule was noticeably drawn out. Once they'd finished saying hello, they went back into

175

the dining room together, talking all the time. I didn't bother to follow them all the way, it would only have drawn attention."

Frey sat for quite a while in silence. He no longer looked irritated, but he was deep in thought. Gudrun huddled up on her end of the simple but elegant-looking wooden bench in the middle of the Vreten underground station. Even from close by, they looked like two strangers waiting for a train, carefully ensuring that the distance between them did not get too intimate. Only when the rails started to buzz did Frey get to his feet.

"There must be a link," he said.

He took a step toward Gudrun, and now it was obvious to anyone watching that they were more than just casual acquaintances.

"I'm going to find out what's going on," he said. "But I've got to do it on my own. From now on, you're off the case."

She raised her head and looked up at him with that compliant look of hers which revealed nothing of the disobedience and protest she could not allow herself to show.

"You know where to find me," she said softly.

"I'll be in touch next week," he said, and left.

As he got on the train, it seemed to her he looked rather more tired than usual. He even waved to her through the carriage window. It was a departure from their strict rules of absolute and constant caution, and one she appreciated.

Perhaps there were a few pieces of Frey's jigsaw puzzle still missing. It would never be complete, but the gaps were not so big that the pattern could not be discerned. Even if a few details were incomplete and blurred the picture, the outline was clear enough.

Frey had good reason to be worried. It was quite clear that, for a long time, Gerd had been dividing her loyalty between him and Dimitri Gusov, that she had been playing a double game. It made no difference that Frey was on the same side as the Russian, in a manner of speaking: Gerd had betrayed her trust. She had let him down and made herself into a threat. Anyone who serves two masters is always ready to serve a third, and that sort of vermin has to be rendered harmless. It was not Frey who had made up the rules. They were accepted everywhere, both in the East and in the West, and they had been current since time immemorial despite the fact that they had never been written down. They were simple, easily understood, and rigorous. All treachery must be punished—immediately. Every indication or suspicion of betrayal must be taken seriously and dealt with straightaway by the invisible tribunal, which passed its irrevocable judgments in accordance with the maxim that it is always safer and more rational to find someone guilty than to let him go free. There is no room for mistakes in the world of secret agents.

History if full of well-loved heroes. Most of them are murderers. A long time ago people used to do their own murders and return in triumph; nowadays they always use henchmen or henchwomen to do the dirty work for them. The bosses of the world's intelligence services always take the credit when things go well. They usually shun the limelight and shy away from publicity, but they know that real honor is only to be found in history, and that it is there their names will be revealed and remembered.

Their equipment, the men who actually carry out their orders, live risky lives in every respect. They are sometimes caught and executed, or are condemned to live for many years in solitary confinement in cells that are more like bunkers. It is less common for them to be caught out by someone more secure and quicker to act than themselves, someone who makes sure they die at the scene of the crime. As they are generally professionals, it needs great carelessness or bad luck for them to be afflicted with one of these

177

alternatives. They run the biggest risk from their own side. Heroes do not want living witnesses of their misdeeds.

It really was not an honorable mission Frey had become involved in.

When a crucial moment full of drama and danger is imminent, most people react by being restless. Although a new wave of snowstorms drifted in over Stockholm that night, several people's temperature rose by several degrees. Most of those involved had only a limited idea of who the others were. Strangely enough, most of them would never get to know each other.

Gerd Angerbo spent the evening and the night in Alf Skolle's apartment. He had surprised her by coming home early, at four in the afternoon, only half an hour or so after she had got back herself. She lied to him and maintained she had not left the apartment all day, apart from a brief excursion to the nearby shops. He believed her, as she had managed to remove her makeup and change; she was wearing his baggy tracksuit bottoms and a colorful sports shirt when he arrived.

"You're early," she said with a broad smile.

She was very pleased with herself. She had been foreseeing and clever. Changing her clothes meant she did not have to explain what she had been doing earlier in the day. Gusov had been very insistent that their meeting should not be known to anyone, especially not to Skolle. The Russian was right. Skolle was unsuspecting by nature.

"The boss sent me home," said Skolle. "He was worried about my health, and concerned that I had got out of bed too soon. He wants me to be in the best of health and sharp as a needle tomorrow. I'm due to see the minister tomorrow afternoon for an important meeting. The section head stressed that it was something very sensitive, and as he knows the minister sets great store by my opinions, he was keen that I should be present. There'll just be the three of us."

"He didn't give any indication of what it was all about, then?"

Skolle shook his head and smiled superciliously. He looked almost statesmanlike.

"We never discuss state secrets in advance," he replied.

"Could it be the memorandum?"

The tense curiosity in her expression was put on; Gusov had already told her the memorandum would be sent to the ministry the next day.

"It could well be," said Skolle. "The section head said something about my knowledge of the Eastern bloc countries being useful."

"What time is the meeting?"

"About four. The minister has another meeting at half past five somewhere in the parliament building. My boss will be going to that, but not me. He did ask me to go with them, though."

Everything Gusov had said was turning out to be correct. His information was surprisingly accurate.

"Do you think you'll get a chance to study the memo on your own?" she asked.

"That's impossible to say. The odds could be better, but it's by no means out of the question."

One hundred and fifty thousand kronor was at stake. Twenty-five thousand for Skolle, and a hundred and twenty-five to Gerd Angerbo. This gamble was different from all others in that the stakes consisted of keeping the winning voucher secret if coincidence, chance, and luck proved to be on their side. All gamblers take risks, and it is not unusual for them to stake their own existence. For Gerd Angerbo and Alf Skolle, the biggest risk was actually being caught in possession of the winning voucher. Only when they had handed it over to the foreign cashier, who has promised to cash it, could they breathe again.

"We must agree about where to meet," said Gerd.

Skolle nodded. He was very serious, and his face had

turned pale. The climax was getting closer, and he was starting to realize that for a few stressful hours the next day, he would be carrying the most serious of incriminating evidence around in his jacket pocket.

"I must get rid of that damned camera as quickly as possible," he said vehemently. "Can you imagine what it feels like to walk around with a time bomb rattling against your side?"

"You have to pass it on to me," said Gerd calmly.

There was no strong liquor in the apartment. Neither Alf nor Gerd had bought any. When they parted that morning, they had agreed in passing that the evening would be a sober one. It had seemed very sensible at the time, but now, eight hours later, Skolle could feel the anger and helplessness beginning to take possession of him. Damned woman!

Just as she was beginning to fear he would lapse into one of his pointless bouts of rage, she noticed his gaze attach itself to the glass-fronted cupboard next to the television set. There, right at the top, next to some idiotic souvenirs of a trip to Italy, were four miniature bottles of liqueur he had forgotten about. Salvation beckoned.

Gerd breathed a sigh of relief. Perhaps it had been a mistake on her part to expect him to get through the evening without a drink. She considered herself to be quite capable of doing without alcohol, and when Skolle opened the first bottle, she had to strain herself so as not to show her contempt. She was not in the least surprised that he did not ask her to share his salvation with him.

He drank cautiously, sipping away like ladies at a tea party. There was nothing else in the house, apart from three bottles of low-alcohol beer in the fridge. The moment he tasted the first, burning drops of the strongly perfumed liqueur on his tongue, he had regained his composure.

"We must decide where to meet," repeated Gerd.

"There's only one possibility," he said quickly. "You'll have to come to the Riksdag building tomorrow evening."

It was an exposed place, but it did have an advantage Skolle did not know about, and which Gerd had no intention of telling him. Gusov had fixed a meeting place for himself and her quite close by.

"Isn't there another entrance at the back?" she asked cautiously. "Isn't the street called Riksgatan?"

"Yes, of course." His face lit up. "That's an excellent suggestion," he said. "A lot of the people who work there prefer to use that very door. It's a bit more anonymous than the fancy main entrance. As I'm in the trade, as it were, I've been told the code to the electronic lock."

"What about security?"

"All the checks are inside the building. Let's face it, the street is one of the main routes for pedestrians to get between the town center and the Old Town. In any case, SÄPO's interest in protecting MPs and other odds and sods like me is regrettably limited."

She was not entirely convinced—far too many television cameras had started to appear in parts of the town. She'd seen lots of them herself when she was out for a stroll.

"I can't hang about there waiting," said Gerd. "You can see that, can't you?"

He nodded.

"It must look as if we've met by accident or, preferably, as if we haven't actually met at all."

"If you've got your handbag open we don't even need to say anything to each other," Skolle pointed out.

There was just one more thing to fix: the timing of the meeting. This had suddenly become vitally important to Gerd.

"It's probable it'll be in the evening. How about twenty to seven?"

She looked expectantly at him.

Skolle hesitated, stroking his chin. Then he opened the second bottle of liqueur and poured the bright purple liquid into his glass. Raising his glass as if to toast her, like an experienced man of the world, he smiled. "Agreed," he said. He looked most surprised when she burst out giggling. "What's so funny?"

"Nothing's funny," replied Gerd. "It's just the tension. By this time tomorrow it'll all be over."

She was celebrating her second stroke of luck that evening. Provided Skolle was not late she would have five minutes in which to get to the meeting place where Gusov would be waiting to take over responsibility for the camera. It could be done. If she did not get there in time, she would have to wait another three hours before she could hand over the little camera, no more than four inches long, with its incriminating contents. Gerd had always been meticulous when it came to keeping appointments, and she hated having to use backup arrangements.

"It's nice to see we can agree so easily," she said. "All we have to do now is synchronize our watches. It's important that you should emerge through that door at exactly the right moment."

"I'll be on time," said Skolle.

End of conversation. It was as if they had no more to say to each other, apart from trivialities and the kind of encouraging words established married couples generally spend the evenings exchanging. Before they went to bed at about half past ten—in their separate rooms as a matter of course, without hiding behind strained excuses—they ran through the timetable once again.

"I'm afraid we won't be able to celebrate our success in the style it deserves," said Skolle. "The champagne will have to wait till I get home. I'm already booked. The section head wants to have dinner with me after the parliament meeting, and you just can't turn down an invitation like that when you're a junior member of the staff."

Moments of clear-sightedness can come at the most inappropriate times. When she was alone in her bedroom, Gerd suddenly got the feeling that something was not quite right. It had all been too easy. Could Gusov and Skolle have planned it all in advance? That was an absurd idea. They did know each other, it was true, but on the few occasions she and Skolle had talked about the Russian and actually named him, he had always been dismissive. As far as Gusov was concerned, he had always been very insistent about how important it was not to tell Skolle who her contact was.

Gerd dismissed the uncomfortable thought. Instead, she took out her paper and pencil and started to do her sums. The total she arrived at was almost half a million. It was no exaggeration to call her well-off. When she turned out the light and closed her eyes, she started to dream about America.

Gudrun Brunhildson did not believe in omens, ghosts, or premonitions. There again, she never denied that she had a sixth sense which sometimes helped her to sniff out danger before it happened.

She was sure she was being followed. Earlier in the day she had the feeling someone was watching her, but now she was certain, although she had no proof, not even a hint of proof.

Her conversation with Frey at Vreten station had lasted for ten minutes, and for most of the time they had been on their own. As the platform began to fill up again, she was convinced that all the faces she scrutinized were new ones, and that none of them had got off the train together with her. Nevertheless, she could not shake off the feeling that she was being followed. There was only one thing to do if she wanted to be certain, and she made up her mind to set a trap.

She had originally intended to go to the Central Station, but instead decided to get off at Fridhelmsplan, an interchange station with exits in all four directions, the least used being the one leading out onto Drottningholmsvägen. During the winter the upper level is usually a gathering point for vagrants, meths drinkers, junkies, and straightforward winos—in short, the dropouts no respectable person wants anything to do with, or even wants to acknowledge their existence. The authorities are equally grudging, and do not even let them take advantage of the little bit of heat they can find in there, even if it is twenty below outside. That is why there are always two guards on duty upstairs, but in spite of their protective presence, most respectable citizens living in that part of town always choose another exit except during the rush hour.

Gudrun did not appear to be in much of a hurry when she got off the train, but neither did she seem especially dilatory. She was one of the last in the stream of people marching through the underground labyrinth. Fridhelmsplan station is very deep, and the escalator there is one of the longest in town. When there were only a few more feet to go, she turned around and looked down behind her: There was no one following her.

She waited outside the barrier for several minutes until she was accosted by an excited and distinctly tipsy woman; the police were busy evicting her equally drunken man, and she was screeching her head off.

"What a goddamned rotten world this is," she yelled. "Police state, that's what it is."

Her black, matted hair straggled down over her cheeks, and her bloodshot eyes filled with tears imploring justice and understanding.

"How are we going to get to Hökarängen now?" she screamed.

"Rubbish!" shouted one of the guards, who was on the spot the moment he heard the scream. Taking firm hold of her arm, he dragged her out into the street. Although she was kicking and scratching and drowning him in a flood of colorful curses, she stood no chance of getting away.

The guard returned, grinning broadly. He felt he had to explain.

"They live in Arbetaregatan, the pair of 'em," he said,

184

spitting on the floor. "That's just around the corner from here. We're always having trouble with them bastards. This is the third time this week I've had to kick 'em out."

Gudrun smiled discreetly at him, and decided it was time to leave the station. It looked as though she had been wrong after all. There was obviously no one tailing her. As she passed through the swinging doors into the street, she almost collided with a short, middle-aged man she thought she recognized. His childish moon-face, and the colorful knitted cap that seemed to emphasize his good hearted smile, seemed familiar. She watched him continue to the barrier and show his monthly season ticket before disappearing into the station.

Only when she was halfway down Hantverkargatan and could make out the City Hall through the snow did she manage to dredge him up from her memory. It was the very same man who had been shoveling snow and sweating away outside Frey's apartment the same afternoon she had returned from her skiing trip to Lake Råsta. She was not quite sure whether she had seen him once or twice more during the past week, but no matter how hard she tried, she could not come up with anything concrete. It was as if he were just managing to dodge her all the time.

She thought for a while, weighing the pros and cons, then shook her head. It was all too improbable. Even though it was always advisable to query the spontaneity of coincidence, and to assume there was a skillful illusionist behind what seemed to be chance, it was just as important to avoid being sidetracked and lured into what turns out to be a cul-de-sac. Every deviation from the stereotyped pattern in the world around us need not constitute a threat. The biggest potential weakness of a secret agent and his organization is paranoid suspicion that never rests. Far too much time, energy, and money are spent on pointless and, as it is easy to see with hindsight, futile pursuits.

It does sometimes happen that one keeps bumping into

the same unknown person again and again until one has the impression one knows him or her. The man with the childlike moon-face presumably lived near Frey, and this last week she had spent many a long hour outside his front door, carefully scrutinizing the face of every passerby. There was a shop in the building, and also an underground station; of the thousand or so men and women she had seen, several of them must have passed by more than once. It was predictable rather than coincidental that she should see some of these faces in some other place as well. Come to that, it was perfectly natural for anybody living in Sundbyberg to catch an underground train at Fridhelmsplan. Even one's sixth sense can be wrong occasionally, she thought to herself, can't it?

Although she was relieved now that common sense had got the better of her occupationally induced paranoia, she felt drained, depressed, and uncomprehending. The game was over—at least as far as she was concerned. She had decided to defy Frey's orders and not stay at home. It was not the fact that she knew what was going to happen which made her worried and restless—she had no moral scruples in the strict meaning of the phrase. A long time ago she had accepted the consequences of the life she had chosen to lead, once and for all. She regarded herself as a soldier at war, and like all soldiers she hated the grenades that landed near her, but not those that killed off the enemy.

Gudrun had lost Klammer, and could see no point in continuing to trail either Gerd Angerbo or Alf Skolle. The only thing that still seemed to make sense was to keep an eye on Frey's apartment.

It was a tired decision, an attempt to convince herself that she could still be of use. What she never admitted was that she could not bear to listen to the neighbors prattling away in the laundry or letting her into intimate secrets over a cup of coffee in her kitchen. Gudrun Brunhildson was nervous, possibly even scared; but she refused to admit it, not even to herself.

She had a snack at the restaurant in the Central Station. The people all around her had such naive expressions on their faces, and the snippets of conversation she managed to pick up were trivial and empty. All she could feel was exhaustion. An hour later she was standing in the taxi queue, slightly drunk, but not so that anyone would notice. There was a faraway look in her eyes. Gudrun Brunhildson was dreaming about tumbling into bed at long last, and waking up the next morning after a long night's peaceful sleep.

That night there were many people busy working away, and looking forward to the next day either in fear and trembling, or with great expectations.

The section head was at a conference that did not end until nearly midnight. For various reasons he had omitted to inform his press secretary, Alf Skolle, about the meeting. When it was finally time to pack up, he was looked very pleased and took his time over saying goodnight, wishing everyone present, including himself, the very best of luck for the coming day. One of the people he had been talking to was the head of the Swedish security services.

The commercial attaché, Dimitri Gusov, Ph.D. (Eng.), had domestic chores to attend to. He was busy packing, and did not finish until two in the morning. Packing cases and cardboard boxes were crammed full of all the things a Soviet citizen feels he should take with him when he returns to the fatherland. There were no brochures in Dr. Gusov's luggage, nothing at all connected with his technical interests, but he did stow away in his diplomatic bag, with great care, a little collection of portraits. It consisted of ten or so photographs of men and women who had meant a lot to him during the many years he had spent in Sweden. Every photo had notes on the back, but apart from the name of the person in the

187

picture, written in the Western alphabet, the combination of letters and figures was opaque to the uninitiated.

Herwart Klammer did not get back to Sundbyberg until three in the morning. He had also said his farewells. Some days previously he had finally managed to find a bar where the clientele consisted exclusively of young boys and elderly gentlemen who liked nothing better than to seduce them. He was accepted straightaway. An eighteen-year-old, a genuine blond Adonis, had enchanted him and taken him back to his luxurious two-room apartment. Klammer would never forget those nights. They had made love, watched videos, studied pictures, then made love once more. It was as if he had tasted freedom for the first time in his life. There had been no pretense between him and the boy. For once he had been able to live out his sexuality without the fear of being found out.

That had not always been the case. Even if he always used to seek out the same experience the night before a critical mission, it had usually turned out to be a squalid affair. The important thing was that he had been able to share his manliness with someone who knew how to appreciate it, even if it had cost him a lot of money.

Klammer felt composed and full of confidence with regard to the next day's action. The only nagging worry, which he tried hard to ignore, was the implications of a word that kept floating into his mind on the way home: AIDS. He suppressed it, just as he suppressed all irrelevant thoughts. Klammer had always had the knack of concentrating exclusively on the task at hand. His bureaucratic mind had no room for questions, profundities, or doubts. The only moral code he recognized was that imposed by his masters.

Frey could hear the guest room wall when Klammer got back to the apartment. He found it difficult to get to sleep, and was sitting in the dark with a glass of whiskey in front of him and a cigarette in his hand. He smiled rather maliciously when he gathered from the noise that the German had taken out his pistol, a Czech CZ-75 with silencer, which had been in the bottom of his suitcase all the time. Frey had known about it since the early days of Klammer's stay.

When the thin beam of light shining in through the crack in the guest room door eventually went out, Frey also went to bed. He felt beaten, and for the first time he had some idea of how a lifer must feel. No freedom, no way out, no choice. They had clapped him in chains he would never be able to cast off. It was as if he had lost his own identity.

16

At about four in the afternoon, Dimitri Gusov left his apartment in the Gärdet suburb and emerged into the street. He was wearing a voluminous Russian fur coat, a similarly impressive fur hat, and to be on the safe side, he had a brilliant red woolen scarf wrapped around his neck. He looked strikingly foreign. He was also wearing a pair of overshoes that, useful though they may be, are no longer in fashion and difficult to find in Swedish shops.

White hell had broken loose, and avalanches of snow were falling over Stockholm. The forecasters had predicted this would happen, and everyone who could had taken the opportunity of going home from work early in order to avoid the inevitable traffic chaos. The center of town was almost devoid of private cars, and although a few accidents blocked some roads and delayed the evacuation, police headquarters was relieved to find, a few hours later, that Stockholm was just as deserted that Friday evening as on Midsummer Day's morning.

The snowstorm reminded Gusov of Moscow. He stood

on the pavement, watching the silent snowflakes as they drifted down, landed gently on his cheeks, and turned into tears. He did so on purpose, not just for sentimental reasons. He was occasionally afflicted by homesickness, but he never allowed it to affect him: Gusov was not the nostalgic type. What he was looking forward to was the freedom of being at home, freedom from the watchful eyes he knew would be following him that evening.

A hundred yards or so away in each direction was a parked car. The snowstorm prevented him from being able to make out details from so far away, but that did not matter: He was convinced there would be two, perhaps even three people in each car, and that they were in communication with each other. Their topic of conversation that evening would be himself. He was not in the least surprised, either, to note the presence of two sportily clad men talking away eagerly in an entranceway a few blocks down the street.

Gusov smiled. It was an amiable smile indicating he approved of the arrangements. The weather was to his liking as well, despite the fact that he was about to set out on a longish trip into the Swedish capital and its suburbs. He was well aware he would be followed by several discreet persons that evening. The snowstorm meant they would have to come closer than he had originally reckoned with, but that was no problem as far as he was concerned. On the contrary, they were the ones who would have difficulties to surmount, and it would put their professional skills to the test. It was in their interests not to lose him under any circumstances, but at the same time, they would have to make sure he had no idea they were there.

In an hour or so, he would make his first attempt to shake off his shadows. He would do it in an unexpected but professional way, but even so, he would fail. He would then try again an hour later, more skillfully this time, but not so successfully that he would manage to get away. Both maneuvers would keep his followers happy, as they would quite reasonably assume he was acting in accordance with set security routines; they would also conclude he was convinced no one was following him.

Gusov took the underground from Karlaplan, and got off at Hötorget. He went straight into PUB—a department store every Russian who visits Stockholm just has to visit. Indeed, it is of historical importance to them, since on one of his prerevolutionary visits to the Swedish capital, Lenin went there to buy a high-quality Swedish replacement for his worn-out Swiss-made suit.

The two sporty gentlemen had now been relieved. It was a quick change. When Gusov paused for a few moments outside one of the few remaining pornography shops in that part of town, he noted that he was now being accompanied by an obviously married couple who turned into the same alley as he had chosen, albeit some distance behind. Both the man and the woman were carrying large plastic carrier-bags, and he could see an aerial sticking up out of one of them. That was careless, even if Stockholm was full of people filling their ears with taped pop music in an attempt to escape from reality.

At the bar in Central Station, Gusov indulged himself with a vodka and a pint of beer. He would miss Swedish beer. To his taste, it was several classes better than Russian beer. Unusual for him, he decided to sit at the bar, and managed to squeeze himself onto a stool between a talkative American and a dour Finn. When he said a few words in Russian, the American fell silent, while the Finn merely raised an eyebrow.

Gusov's seat meant that he had turned his back on most of the customers, thus making it easier for the people trailing him to keep an eye on him. A few minutes later Gusov was pleased to see in the mirror that the man with the radio had separated from the woman. It did not take too much of a wild guess to conclude that she was resting her weary feet on a bench in the waiting room, keeping an eye on the restaurant entrance at the same time.

Shortly afterward Gusov made his first attempt to get away from his shadows. Like all the rest of the customers, he had left his outer clothes in the cloakroom leading straight out into the concourse. At first it looked as though he was going to retrace his steps; then it seemed as if he were hesitating to join the mass of people tramping angrily up and down, waiting for their delayed train to be announced by the loudspeakers at long last.

Quite unexpectedly he suddenly turned around. A little queue had formed around the cloakroom attendant, and as Gusov forced his way through the queue he happened to bump into the man he had just been watching in the mirror. He muttered a few incomprehensible words of apology and received a few equally incomprehensible mutters in return. Both men avoided looking the other in the eye. He then speeded up and half ran, fur coat and all, through the bar and into the oblong dining room, which was done out like a turn-of-the-century dining car. There is an entrance there from Vasagatan that most Stockholmers do not think about, and people from the provinces do not know about. Gusov deserved high marks for local knowledge by choosing that exit for his getaway attempt.

Without slowing down, Gusov rushed past the taxi queue outside the Central Station. He slid about in the slush, but managed to stay on his feet with his red scarf fluttering in the breeze. He was out of breath by the time he reached the eastern underground entrance opposite the main post office. Without looking around he raced down the stairs, but lost several seconds at the barrier as he was forced to take out his wallet in order to pay for his ticket. He was remarkably clumsy. He did not bother to look around: There should be somebody behind him all right. At least one car had followed him as he careened down Vasagatan.

The underground labyrinth constituting the heart of the

Stockholm underground and known as T-Centralen was crowded with people. Moisture was dripping from walls and ceilings, passages and staircases were dirty and treacherous, handrails as slippery as eels. Shallow pools of melted snow had formed on the platforms. The storm had not penetrated as far down as this, but its influence was felt everywhere. Everybody's face was blank and expressionless, their collars and hats dripping with water, and the smell of damp clothing was all-pervading.

Everything was happening at high speed, as everyone made haste to get home as quickly as possible. It was only natural. Blazing fires, warm rooms, four walls, the security of the family were the only sure protection from the icy winds now blasting the country. Hence it was more important than ever not to miss the train, despite the fact that hardly anybody knew the timetable by heart or even paused to think what time it was. There were no clashes or bottlenecks. Discipline was good, and anyone unable to keep up with the increased speed stuck close to the walls or clung tightly to the handrail on the escalators.

Gusov adjusted his speed to that of the masses. He knew it would be a blatant mistake to try and elbow his way through the crowd. Anyone running is always easier to spot than somebody quietly maintaining his due place in the apparently endless stream of faceless humanity flowing along in the same direction. That is not the way a specially trained secret agent behaves. It is a sign of fear or panic, reactions one does not expect of a hardened KGB officer. Gusov was just behind a group of young people, forcing their way through whenever they came across any kind of obstacle, and hard on his heels was a broad-shouldered giant of a man in a large parka. An excellent shield against inquiring looks from the rear.

For a brief while he was afraid he might have been all too successful in his efforts to get clear, but he was lucky. Having reached the platform, he had to wait several minutes before the Mörby train arrived, and there was nowhere to hide. One or two of the Stockholmers on their way home cast jealous glances at his elegant Russian fur coat. If Gusov had made any mistake at all, it was in his choice of clothes.

Gusov clambered into a car in the middle of the train. He was one of the last through the doors, and was forced to stand for the first part of the journey, trying to keep upright and clinging onto the rail. He was not particularly worried, as he was sure he had company once more.

All occupations make their mark on the people concerned. Anybody can point out a rock blaster, a fashion model, or a miserable-looking magistrate in a crowd of people. For the uninitiated, however, it might be more difficult to pick out a police sleuth, as they are usually very good at assuming everyday disguises. For someone like Dr. Gusov, with his long experience of police and security agents in all parts of the world, it was not an impossible task.

He now had two new guardian angels. One was lanky, with the face of an aesthetic gravedigger. It was his eyes that gave him away: They were alert but cold, appraising, totally lacking in frivolity, and as desolately lonely and rejected as only a policeman's eyes can be. The other man was a more jovial type, but he, too, was betrayed by his eyes. He smiled with his face and his lips, but his eyes remained cold and alert, quick to assess, and strangely hostile to any attempt at making contact. There was also a bulge in his ski jacket just under his left shoulder, indicating that he was wearing a shoulder-holster.

The man with the face of a gravedigger was in the car in front of Dr. Gusov's, while the other was in the one behind. The Russian had a cunning expression on his face—so far, everything had gone according to plan.

Mörby station is a terminus, and all the passengers still aboard left the train quickly. Only Gusov lingered behind. For a while it looked as though he was thinking of going back to where he had come from, using the same route and the same

195

train, but he was ordered off by the driver, who pointed out that passengers were not allowed in a train when it was shunting. With evident reluctance he wandered off toward the escalator, glancing around him unobtrusively at the same time. There was no sign of his guardian angels.

Half an hour later Dr. Gusov was pacing nervously back and forth beside the taxi stand at Mörby. He had to wait quite a while, and it looked as if he were starting to run short of time. He kept taking off his glove and drawing back his left sleeve to check his watch. He had not been seen in any of the shops at the Mörby complex, but he had taken a great interest in the floors devoted to parking. He had also used the elevator several times, and among other things had taken a good look at the offices at the top of the building. Although he looked restless, he showed no sign of suspecting that he was being followed.

One of SÄPO's cars was waiting for him as his taxi pulled away from the Mörby complex. It emerged rather too quickly from the gas station opposite, but it soon put that mistake right: Dr. Gusov nodded in approval as it overtook his taxi. Despite the snow, once they were out on the motorway, Gusov could see that another car was following behind. When they got to Berghamra, he ordered the driver to turn right and approach the Stockholm city center via Solna. The driver muttered something scathing about crazy foreigners but did as he was bidden. Just as he had feared, there were about six inches of snow on Sjövägen, and hardly any sign of tire tracks. The way they failed to clear the snow in this area had always been disgraceful. He had to reduce speed to not much more than ten miles an hour, and when Gusov checked the back window, he could see they had company. Two more cars had taken this decidedly unreliable route into Stockholm.

Gusov sat back in the rear seat, smiling. He was very pleased with himself. His escort was having a few problems just now, that was true, but he was sure they could cope. All was going according to plan, and he had plenty of time. The only real risk he had taken was the possibility of SÄPO not getting cars to Mörby in the twenty minutes available, but he had not overestimated the efficiency of the Swedish security services. He had always rated them highly as far as technical problems were concerned.

The taxi came to a halt opposite the statue of Gustav III at Skeppsbron Bridge. The blizzard was as bad as ever, and the wind had increased. It was real Siberian weather, and quite unfit for evening strolls. Despite his fur hat and thick fur coat, the Russian could feel the cold beginning to get to him. The sentry outside the palace courtyard was trying in vain to seek adequate shelter in his tiny box, and apart from him, it was hard to find any signs of life.

As he continued deeper into the Old Town, Gusov came across several bleak-looking figures struggling along as near to the house walls as possible in order to try and escape the driving winds. Gusov now seemed to have a spring in his step and was walking more purposefully than before. He proceeded along a sort of zigzag route through the streets and alleys, and sometimes turned about to retrace his steps. When he came to Västerlånggatan, where a thin line of pedestrians were struggling along against the storm, he looked carefully around in all directions, then crossed rapidly over the well-lit shopping street and turned into Tyska brinken. Then he disappeared.

The owner of the Hungarian basement-restaurant in Tyska Brinken was very pleased to see his Russian guest and immediately served him a glass of hot red-wine toddy on the house—he could no doubt do with it after struggling with the cold outside. The landlord had only just opened. It was ten past six, and Dr. Gusov was the first customer of the night. As he studied the menu—he was contemplating a well-spiced goulash for his main course, and pancakes with chocolate sauce for dessert—the little cloakroom filled up with new customers. It was impossible not to see what kind of people they were.

The restaurant was divided into two parts, and Gusov had chosen to sit in one corner of the outer room. He was not in the least surprised when the first set of new arrivals refrained from keeping him company and instead continued through to the inner room. Over the next ten minutes or so, more new customers arrived. Some of them looked like ordinary Stockholmers, including a young couple who seemed to be very much in love, and three women of pensionable age who were very talkative and appeared to have primed themselves for a jolly evening. The next group, however, three men and a woman, were very discreet and, although the landlord gestured them toward a table farther into the dining room, they preferred to sit next to the entrance.

Twenty minutes later, at six-forty to be exact, Dimitri Gusov was served a bowl of piping hot and very tasty goulash. He was very much aware of the time. As far as he could see, all the cars SÄPO could muster should have converged on the Old Town by now. Some of them would definitely be guarding the roads leading off the island, and the rest would be parked near the restaurant. Only a few of the police on duty would need to be out struggling with the weather. The Swedish security forces were getting ready for their biggest coup of all time. Not only were they going to expose and arrest one of the most important spies in the history of Sweden together with his female accomplice, but they would also catch red-handed the Russian diplomat who was their contact and controller. It was a feat that would be emblazoned across the front pages of the world's press as an enormous sensation, and that evening's events in Stockholm would make SÄPO secure for some considerable time to come.

Alf Skolle had a strenuous and nerve-racking day, but on the whole, it had gone well. Some of his colleagues noticed he was quieter than usual, and that he kept to himself in his office. They assumed it was the aftereffects of his influenza, and that it would be a few more days before he was completely restored to normal health.

At about three he was called in to the minister in order to go through the secret memorandum about the complicated questions concerning the border dispute in the Baltic that had just been sent over from the prime minister's office. Together with the section head, they had discussed the consequences a firm stand would have for trade. After an hour of discussions the minister had asked his colleagues to draft a response summarizing the points they had made. They withdrew to the section head's office and continued their discussions for another half an hour, at which point the section head rose to his feet and patted Skolle on the shoulder.

"I'll leave you in peace and quiet so you can be getting on with it," he said. "You'll have to write the draft in here as the document is not allowed to leave my office."

He paused in the doorway and smiled with surprising warmth.

"You've got three quarters of an hour," he said. "Then we'll have to be going to parliament. Don't forget we've agreed to have dinner later on."

Gerd Angerbo had been surprised by the blizzard, and although she was dressed for winter, she would have preferred less elegant but warmer clothes. She was nervous, but not noticeably on edge. It was not because of nerves that she had decided to stop in at the Opera Bar for a drink: She was far too early and, in addition, it would look odd if she insisted on walking around outdoors.

To her relief there was not a single face she recognized in the bar. She was one of the majority who preferred the rather more frivolous atmosphere of the café on the ground floor— she had never felt she had much in common with the cultured and quasi-intellectual frequenters of the Opera Bar.

There was plenty of room that evening—even the regulars were put off by the snowstorm. No one bothered her, but she could not help noticing she aroused a certain amount of curiosity. As she was keeping herself aloof, even those who needed the bar to prop them up soon grew tired of her, and tomorrow, they would not even remember what she looked like.

At a quarter past six she paid her bill, but she didn't leave immediately. She reckoned she had a five-minute walk ahead of her, perhaps six in view of the blizzard. As she left the premises the clock in St. Jacob's Church struck half past six. On no account must she arrive too soon, so she paused at the Bakfickan restaurant and examined the menu. This was where the artistes from the Opera House generally went when they were feeling peckish.

When she looked around she noticed two men coming rapidly toward her from the corner of Fredsgatan. It looked as though they were a little startled to see her, but after only a hint of hesitation they kept on walking and were deep in conversation as they went past. She recognized them immediately—they had been at the same table in the Opera Bar. She thought hard for a moment and tried to remember: Had they been there when she arrived, or had they come later? She could not quite remember.

All afternoon she had been very careful to check whether anyone had displayed any special interest in her. When she had decided to go to the Opera Bar she was a hundred percent certain no one was tailing her. After all, why should anybody want to? She must not lose her composure or start seeing ghosts in the snow whirling all around her. The crucial moment was approaching. At last, she would be rid of Alf Skolle and Dimitri Gusov. The stakes were high, but the odds were more than satisfactory. Next week she would be rich and thus in a position to leave the country. What was it that Frey was always telling her? The greatest danger for a secret agent is fear. He usually added that an agent's greatest opponent is his imagination. On the other hand, she remembered that he also used to say a secret agent who can no longer manage to be suspicious of everybody and everything is not only a burned-out agent but also a dead one.

She clenched her teeth. The time was up. After this she would be free, once and for all.

Gerd crossed over Gustav Adolf's Square and continued toward Riksbron Bridge over Strömgatan. The light was still on in some windows of the Crown Prince's Palace, where Sweden's foreign affairs were sorted out. Despite the severe cold, the water was racing and bubbling along the Norrström channel as she paused in the middle of the bridge to check the time. It looked as though she was watching the creaking chunks of ice dancing down the channel. Two minutes to go, and she was starting to count the seconds. She could not see anything suspicious behind her: Drottninggatan was more or less deserted. A hundred yards or so ahead of her, she could just make out the backs of the two men from the Opera Bar. They were on their way to the Old Town. The last she saw of them was that one turned around.

The door leading out of the parliament building opened when she was still fifteen yards away. Alf Skolle emerged into the street. He had his fur coat on but was bareheaded—typically careless of him, and she felt pangs of irritation. The next moment their eyes met, and she could see the gleam of triumph in his expression. He had done it.

Gerd opened up the already half-open handbag she was carrying in her right hand, and at the same time Skolle took his left hand out of his pocket. Concealed in it was the four-inch-long camera. He unclenched his fist and let the camera fall into her handbag, winking at her as if he had just played some boyish prank. Then he turned on his heel, went back to the door, and punched in the electronic code that would open the lock.

What happened next was very confusing. The reason for the confusion was Gerd Angerbo's behavior. It would be

201

several vital minutes before the security police could be given new orders—they had all converged on the Old Town. Their leaders were convinced the trap was correctly set, and nothing would prevent it from being sprung. They did not have a single car covering the Norrmalm area. All the foot-soldiers had been directed to the Old Town and were centered on Västerlånggatan. Most of them were not actually in the street, in fact—Gerd Angerbo was not to be made suspicious. The two who had been detailed to shadow her were now in front of her, but their orders were just as clear as those of the others: Under no circumstances were they to arouse her suspicions. Everybody was waiting for Gerd to go down the steps into the Hungarian restaurant. That was where they were going to pounce—unexpectedly, surely, and sensationally.

The photographer in charge of the film camera opposite the rear side of the parliament building, on the top floor of the old Bank of Sweden, had shot the whole encounter between Alf Skolle and Gerd Angerbo. He was quite sure he had got everything. As Alf Skolle disappeared through the door, the photographer turned in triumph to his assistant.

"A real bull's-eye," he announced with a grin. "I actually got the camera in his hand as he passed it over."

They congratulated each other, and returned to the window. Although they had only relaxed their vigil for a few seconds, Gerd Angerbo had disappeared from view. They assumed, correctly, that she had crossed over the road.

Alf Skolle had a broad grin on his face as the door closed behind him. He was approached by the security guards, accompanied by two other serious-looking men.

"I forgot my fur hat," he explained cheerfully. "What foul weather!"

"You're not going to need a fur hat for the rest of your life," said one of the serious-looking men.

Skolle stiffened, and when he saw several of them had

pistols in their hands he began to realize what that meant, incredulously at first but then with a feeling of increasing desperation. His first reaction was to protest. Didn't they know who he was? In any case, they had no proof—he had just got rid of that. They could not have anything on him that would hold water in court. Unless . . . Of course! They are arrested Gerd as well. Or . . .

When one of the men put his hand on his shoulder, Skolle gave himself up. It dawned on him, in a flash of terrifying insight, that his plight was hopeless, that he had nothing to cling on to. All was lost.

"In the name of the law," said one of the policemen solemnly, "I arrest you, Alf Skolle, on suspicion of high treason and illegal intelligence activities in the service of a foreign power."

Skolle shook his head.

"You must be out of your minds," he said.

His protest sounded lame and weak even to himself. It was not much more than a whisper. They stared at him, and there was both contempt and respect in their eyes. Then one of the policemen clapped a set of handcuffs onto his right wrist.

Handcuffed, silent, and with tears in his eyes, Skolle offered no resistance and was led through the parliament building to the police car parked outside a side door. The arrest aroused no interest. Even before they drove out of the square in front of parliament, they radioed headquarters with the news that their mission had been completed successfully. Without more ado, they drove straight to HQ in Bergsgatan.

Those in charge of the investigation were informed immediately, and congratulated themselves on their indisputable success. The first phase of the operation had gone according to plan. But half a minute later the mood at headquarters changed dramatically as news came in from the Old Town that they had lost Gerd Angerbo.

* * *

It took Gerd no more than one minute to get to the Drottninggatan and Fredsgatan crossroads. She had ruined all the cleverly laid police plans and carefully considered conclusions by going back the way she had come. It was incomprehensible and illogical, and at first the ones directly responsible in the Old Town refused to take the report seriously. The Russian was sitting in a restaurant surrounded by their people. He was the contract man. That was where she was going. That was where they were going to pounce.

Gerd started walking more briskly as she turned into Fredsgatan and was almost running by the time she was approaching Tegelbacken. Directly opposite one end of the Chancellery is a little street known as Akademigränd; here she made a sharp right turn. She breathed a sigh of relief when she saw the private car standing in front of a workmen's hut on the left side of the street. All was going according to plan.

There were two men in the car, and she saw straightaway that the one at the wheel was not Dimitri Gusov. He must be the one in the back.

The front window was down, and she had taken the camera out of her handbag even before she got there. At the same moment she caught sight of the driver's face.

"You . . . !" she gasped in horror.

It was Frey.

The back door opened, and the man in the backseat leaned forward.

"Miss Angerbo," he said in German, his voice dry and bureaucratic. "I'm the one who should have the camera."

She hesitated for a second and looked inquiringly at Frey. She thought she saw him nod his head, and decided to obey. Why had Gusov changed their plans? This was the first time he had ever sent a substitute. Was it because the material was red hot?

Smiling almost knowingly, she took a step closer to the

man in the backseat and held out the camera. She could barely make him out. The shadow of the workmen's hut and the densely falling snow prevented the light from Jakobsgatan getting through.

The moment she turned to walk away, Klammer shot her three times. Each one of them was fatal. As the third bullet went home, she had already hit the pavement.

"Let's go!" said Klammer.

The muffled sound of a CZ can barely be heard from more than thirty yards away. The silencer, the howling blizzard, and the location in an out-of-the-way little alley combined to make the murder of Gerd Angerbo unnoticed at first. It would be another five minutes before the security police had managed to get to this part of the city from the Old Town, and another seven minutes before two of them almost stumbled over the stiffening body of Gerd Angerbo.

Frey was shaken, but he forced himself into a state of frosty indifference. He transformed himself into a robot with just one aim: to get them away unnoticed from the scene of the murder. Mechanically, he drove into Jakobsgatan and, as expected, had to stop at traffic lights several times as they went along Tegelbacken. He jumped the last set after only fifteen seconds—there was not much traffic about, and in these treacherous conditions no one bothered about minor breaches of the law. The most important thing was to keep an adequate distance behind the car in front. He continued up the hill toward Kungsholmen, and when they had to stop at the lights yet again in Bergsgatan, he could hear the police sirens for the first time. He misunderstood the situation, thinking the murder had already been discovered. But the police car turned off in a different direction, and he was able to drive on undisturbed toward the Klara district, once again ignoring no entry signs and notices claiming, falsely, that the streets were blocked.

Ten minutes later, they were in Sundbyberg.

Klammer got out of the car not far from Frey's apartment,

and only then did they exchange their first words after the murder.

"The films?" asked Frey.

"In safe keeping, all three," replied Klammer.

"I want an explanation."

"Of course. How long will it take you to get back once you've got rid of the car?"

"Twenty minutes, at most."

"Excellent. I have to leave tonight, and if you're not back by eight, we shan't see each other again."

Frey felt his senses slowly returning to normal, and shook his head bitterly. He was not going to get away with it as easily as that.

"I'll be back in time," he said, "and I'm not convinced half an hour's chat will be enough."

"We'll see," said Klammer, calmly.

Watching the German in the mirror, Frey thought he could see him smiling. In any case, he looked very pleased with himself. The bulge in his overcoat pocket showed he had detached the silencer but still had the weapon.

17

The Hallonbergen garage was full of cars, but there was not a soul in sight. Even the children had deserted what had become their sheltered playground after the blizzard had driven them away from the skating rink and sled runs. Families were gathered around dining tables, talking about the storm. Before long they would be sitting in front of their television sets, watching the news.

Frey parked the car exactly where he had found it. If its owner had a look at it the next morning, he might be surprised by the pool of water under the car and the dirty license plates. So much that happens in this life is never fully explained. Only the police technicians would be able to establish whether or not the dark stains on the backseat were caused by gunpowder.

No one saw Frey leave the garage. Unlike most car thieves, he had taken good care of the vehicle and returned it in perfect condition. He had left behind a few insignificant riddles that might be difficult to solve, but no property had been damaged and the whole mystery would soon be forgotten—if indeed it was ever noticed.

He had ten minutes' walk ahead of him, and he took the shortcut through the woods. It felt good, plodding through the snow, and he did not mind the wind blasting into his face. Nature was scourging him, and he gave himself up to be purified. He was not indignant, nor was he calm. He was in full possession of his senses, and was feeling, thinking, and analyzing as usual. And yet he was not himself. He was functioning like a sedated patient in a mental hospital. His emotions were dulled, his aggressions buried deep, and his resistance greatly reduced. It would be several days before he was completely back to normal.

He acknowledged coldly that he had been an accomplice in the execution of Gerd Angerbo, his own agent and occasionally also his mistress. He felt no regret, nor did he feel any guilt. Klammer had maintained she was a traitor and hence must be liquidated, an allegation that was not improbable even though the German had produced no proof. On the other hand, it was irrefutable that Gerd had been working for someone else as well. She had deceived him and let him down, and his attitude toward her had changed fundamentally. She was no longer a woman he could make love to and use of, but also protect: She was a threat that must be eliminated. He acknowledged with a grimace that Klammer had relieved him of a problem he would have found very difficult to solve once and for all himself, inevitable though it might be.

There was a lot Frey still did not understand. He realized of course that there was a link between Gerd Angerbo, Alf Skolle, and Herwart Klammer, and that the Russian was probably involved as well. But just how had she turned traitor? She had handed over a camera, and she had known all about the meeting place and had gone there quite deliberately, only to be murdered. The timing must have been agreed to in advance as well. She had walked straight into the trap without even knowing it was a trap.

They always baited their traps. Frey slowed down as he approached his apartment. Was he being just as naive as Gerd had been? Just what was the mission Klammer had come to Stockholm to carry out? Slowly, Frey began to understand, or at least to catch on. He recalled Gudrun Brunhildson's skiing trip: that was where the key to the whole thing lay. The man Klammer had met on the edge of the woods at Lake Råsta was the main character in the play.

There was only one witness to the murder of Gerd Angerbo. Murderers do not want to know about any living witnesses. Anyone who allows himself to become an accomplice in a murder often runs just as big a risk as the victim. Indifference to human life and utterly ruthless cruelty are just as widespread in the world of secret agents as they are in that of gangsters. The only thing that matters is removing all traces, making an entry in the notebook of history that is never explained.

Frey was unarmed. Up there in his apartment was Herwart Klammer, a professional killer whose cold-blooded efficiency he had observed at close quarters. As Frey took hold of the handle of the outside door, he hesitated. Was he talking with open eyes into a trap that had been set for him? He would have very little chance of resisting if the German had decided to use his weapon one more time. There was just one way out, a necessary and perhaps desperate risk. He must try and disarm Klammer. Immediately, the moment he walked in through the door of his apartment.

Somebody tapped him on the shoulder, and when he turned around he found himself gazing into the serious but friendly face of a middle-aged man he thought he recognized but could not place. He was wearing an old-fashioned overcoat that came down below his knees and partially obscured a pair of surprisingly baggy and fluffy trousers. Frey had made up his mind. He opened the door and walked resolutely toward the elevator with the other man hard on his heels. The elevator was waiting on the ground floor, and Frey opened the door—then froze. Standing in the far corner was a little man with a moon-face and a childlike smile, pointing a pistol at him. It seemed to be far too heavy for his chubby hand. At the same time Frey felt another gun pressed into his back.

"It's loaded," smiled the man in the elevator. "As you're a sensible man, you won't try and do anything silly, will you?"

He spoke slowly and carefully with a foreign accent that might be Baltic.

"You needn't worry," added the little man reassuringly. "We're not going to hurt you. On the contrary, we're doing this for your own good. Sometimes a man has to be protected from himself, and we think you are about to expose yourself to unnecessary danger. If you don't make trouble, no harm will come to you. We'll try and make sure the next few hours are not too uncomfortable for you."

Frey did not answer. He was surprised, almost shocked, and had no idea what was happening. He needed time to get a grip on himself. Despite the two threatening pistols, for some strange reason he felt relieved. As if he had been saved from making a critical mistake. He decided to play for time and do as he was told. Sooner or later he would get an opportunity of recovering his freedom of action.

The elevator traveled only one floor, down to the basement. The man in the buggy trousers was behind Frey all the time. He had put the gun in one of the voluminous pockets of his overcoat, and Frey could occasionally feel it pressing against his buttocks. It was not a deadly threat, but frightening enough to make him keep still.

They stopped in front of the door leading out into the ticket hall of the underground station, the one Frey had considered his safest exit from the building. The anarchistic Austrian had not been satisfied with selling his keys to just one person, and Frey wondered, not without amusement, how many sets he had made.

"Now," said the little man. "We're going to have to cross over the hall outside. This is the critical bit. There could be people there, but they won't be able to help you. The ticket collector is an Arab, and he learned long ago to stay in his little box and never interfere in what Swedes do."

"I understand," said Frey.

There was no sign of anybody in the hall. Not even the Arab. He had left his post, probably to go and have a cup of coffee at the café over the street. They crossed rapidly to the other side of the hall, a strange procession that could have come from a slapstick comedy. There was another door there that Frey had noticed, but he had never wondered where it led to. The moon-faced man took out another key, opened the door, and politely asked Frey to enter first.

Behind the door was a room no more than nine feet square, not much more than a cupboard. The furniture consisted of two shabby armchairs and a stool. In one of the armchairs sat Gudrun Brunhildson, bound and gagged. Her eyes opened wide when she saw Frey, and there was something resigned about her look.

"I know you two are acquainted," said the little man with a smile. "Your girlfriend devotes a lot of energy and concern to your safety. So do we. We have great admiration for you both, and regret very much that we have been forced to take drastic action in this manner."

The door had been closed behind them as soon as they had entered the room, and the man in the baggy trousers was blocking it. He had taken the pistol out of his pocket and was pointing it at Frey.

"If you wouldn't mind," said the other man, pointing toward the empty armchair.

There was no choice. Despite their peculiar appearance and considerate behavior, they were acting with the kind of confidence that indicated they were competent professionals who meant what they said. In less than a minute, Frey was strapped to the armchair with a strip of tape over his mouth. When the moon-faced man, who was still wearing his woolen hat, sat down on the stool in front of them, Frey realized there were only three of them left in the room.

An hour and a half later, a time the three spent in complete silence, the man in the knee-length coat returned.

"He's gone," he announced objectively.

With a satisfied smile, his friend rose from the stool he had been occupying all the time the other man had been out, pistol in hand, but not pointed at his prisoners. With a few simple moves, he loosened the rope binding Gudrun without taking it away altogether.

Then he took two paces back, put the pistol in his pocket, and bowed politely.

"Good-bye," he said. "It has been a great pleasure knowing you."

The next moment, he and his silent companion had disappeared.

It only took Gudrun a minute to untie herself, and she had no difficulty in freeing Frey.

"Do you understand what's going on?" she asked.

"I think so," replied Frey, holding up a matchbox the moon-faced man had left behind on the stool. It had a picture depicting two dragons breathing fire, advertising a Chinese restaurant not far away.

18

The sensational arrest of a major spy in Stockholm by the Swedish security services made the headlines in most Western newspapers. Sales of the evening tabloids in Sweden went up by tens of thousands for several weeks, and relations with the Great Power in the east cooled noticeably for the rest of the year. The long-drawn-out negotiations over the border in the Baltic collapsed yet again.

Alf Skolle admitted without much resistance more or less everything he was accused of. It was only when the case against him opened—he was sentenced to life imprisonment—that he was informed of Gerd Angerbo's murder. Throughout the vigorous interrogation he had always assumed she was alive and under arrest.

To SÄPO's disappointment, Skolle could only tell them about his own activities, which documents he had passed on, and how much money he had received in return. He referred them to Gerd Angerbo on all other matters. He was not even sure who handled her, though he assumed it must be a Russian.

"We just referred to him as *him*," he kept saying in reply

to the chief interrogator's repeated question about who had benefited from Skolle's espionage.

The murder of Gerd Angerbo was never solved, which meant that praise for SÄPO's efforts was qualified, and in time was replaced altogether by a series of critical voices claiming the security services had made an incredible hash of things as usual. Speculation by an unknown free-lance journalist that SÄPO had stumbled into a trap was dismissed as mere speculation and never taken seriously in the debate proper. The Russian embassy denied all involvement, and maintained as usual that the whole story was a disgraceful piece of provocation on the part of Swedish right-wing elements. The Russian protests were greeted by most Swedes with a resigned shrug of the shoulders: What else could you expect from that quarter?

The Russian commercial attaché, Dr. Dimitri Gusov, left as planned the day after Gerd Angerbo's murder, in a sleeping car from Stockholm Central Station to Moscow. The security services asked the Foreign Office if there was any chance of preventing him from leaving the country but were told it could not be done: They had been informed in good time of his impending departure, in accordance with the regulations, and had thanked him officially by inviting him to a farewell dinner at the Riche.

Joans Mikael Frey and Gudrun Brunhildson canceled everything for the immediate future. They spent two very pleasant and happy weeks together on Malta, and returned reasonably well restored in both body and soul.

A few weeks later Frey was summoned to Berlin. The Colonel received him personally, and they spent a pleasant evening together in the Colonel's luxurious mansion at Müggelsee. Toward the end of the evening, encouraged by the amount of vodka he had consumed, the Colonel became more communicative than usual.

"You must realize, old fellow," he said boisterously, "that

I was against this business right from the start. But there's nothing I can do to stop our brothers in Moscow when they come out with these absurd ideas of theirs. Before long the Swedish security services will draw the obvious conclusions. That press secretary was sacrificed in order to prevent their big mole from being exposed. If I understand it rightly, he retires this year and he wants to have a line of retreat open. Sensibly enough, he wants to stay in Sweden.

"Herwart Klammer?" wondered Frey.

"A particularly unpleasant killer," replied the Colonel. "One of the worst type. But the way things had gone in Stockholm, he really did do us a favor. Somehow or other we would have had to do something about Gerd Angerbo."

"Was that why I was involved" asked Frey.

"Of course," said the Colonel. "She came within your sphere of responsibility as well as mine."

In due time everything went back to normal. Secret activities slowly began to take place again just as they had always done, and always will. There was just one man who could not shake off the worry and fear. Herwart Klammer kept waking up in a cold sweat in the middle of the night, increasingly often. It would be many years before he was quite sure whether or not he had been infected.